WILD CHILD ·

CHLOË RAYBAN

D1345053

THE BODLEY HEAD
LONDON

First published in 1991 by
The Bodley Head Children's Books
an imprint of The Random Century Group Ltd
20 Vauxhall Bridge Road, London SW1V 2SA

Random Century Australia Pty Ltd
20 Alfred Street, Sydney, NSW 2061

Random Century New Zealand Ltd
PO Box 40-086, Glenfield, Auckland 10, New Zealand

Random Century South Africa Pty Ltd
PO Box 337, Bergvlei 2012, South Africa

Photoset by SX Composing Ltd, Rayleigh, Essex
Printed and bound by Bookcraft (Bath) Ltd

A catalogue record for this book is
available from the British Library

ISBN 0 370 31674 6

I

I suppose the thought first came to me on the sunbed. Franz's mother had enrolled Franz into this Health and Leisure Club with the idea that she would use it for work-outs in the gym. We used to go there every Friday when we got off early from school. We soon discovered it did a whole lot more for our bodily welfare lazing in the sauna or spending an illicit extra half hour on a sunbed.

On this particular Friday afternoon, Franz and I had managed to get two sunbeds side by side and were having this sort of loud, muffled conversation through their closed lids.

'The only thing is,' said Franz, 'they say if you spend too much time on a sunbed you get all dehydrated and wrinkly—like being over-microwaved and you've dried out the gravy.'

'Gross,' I said. 'Like being middle-aged.'

'Some people are born middle-aged,' observed Franz.

'Like Fiona Ponsonby-Haugh? Hard case,' I agreed.

'Personally, I'm going to end it all long before then,' said Franz.

The echoing sunbed added somewhat to her tone of melodrama.

'Where do you draw the line?' I pointed out. 'Once you're over twenty you might as well resign yourself to the fact you're going to spend *the rest of your life* Grown-Up-and-Past-It.'

The conversation had spread a kind of gloom in the hot enclosed space of the sunbed.

'If it's OK with you I think I'll just take a shower and make for home,' I said.

Franz opened the lid of her sunbed and leaned out. She raised her goggles and stared at me. She had white rings round her eyes where the goggles had been, like a panda in negative.

'But you've only had forty minutes,' she said.

On the way home in the Tube I studied the other people in my carriage. Most of them seemed to be surviving those grey featureless years between youth and oblivion with amazing strength of character. I examined their faces, one by one, as they rocked in patient unison to the rhythm of the train.

There were a couple of the usual secretaries with their velvet Alice-bands and mock Cartier earrings taking home Safeway bags full of taramasalata and ready-to-heat Chicken Kiev to feed their current boyfriends. There was the standard tube-train mad person—a lady with cropped lilac hair muttering to herself and underlining things in strong red Biro in what looked like a library book. There was a not wildly attractive couple who kept putting their arms round each other and nuzzling etc in a valiant effort to reassure themselves they could be classified as lovable. There were a few yuppie executives of both sexes. And there was a phased-out looking dyed blonde holding a sleeping baby and accompanying her Walkman with a tuneless hum. The thing was, they all had the same look on their faces—an expression of blankness, of drabness, of deep suffocating greyness.

And I knew, with a sinking feeling in my stomach and

with the kind of inevitability I simply couldn't ignore, that somewhere—way out there ahead in the future—I was going to be ONE OF THEM.

I also recognised that every one of these people had once been, like me, pure untapped star material—all their lives ahead of them with virtually anything possible. And yet, somehow, they had all Got It Wrong.

All these poor deprived grey people had forgotten what living was like. It made me want to stand up and shout 'WAKE UP'. But luckily I generally have the self-control to resist most of my wilder impulses.

Instead, I started to think about that distant, future me. Did she realize what lay ahead? Did she know that she was in grave danger of the very worst thing that can happen in anyone's life—ABSOLUTELY NOTHING. I mean, just imagine waking up one morning and finding you've allowed yourself to get dull, grey and ordinary and *not having done anything about it!*

I decided I had to warn that future person I was going to become before it was too late. I puzzled over how to do this all the way to Sloane Square. And eventually came up with the only solution I could think of. It was to write myself a letter.

I wrote it as soon as I got home.

It went:

Dear Me,

How I wish that I could actually talk to you face to face. But since I can't I'm writing to you instead.

I want you here and now to solemnly swear that you are never, never going to let yourself get middle-aged and ordinary. (Please be on the watch for the first telltale signs like the urge to wear flesh-coloured tights or feeling lost without a handbag, or starting to cut recipes out of magazines and store them in a ring-binder.)

Whatever happens, I want you to do everything in your power to become famous, someone who gets noticed and gets in the papers. So that one day you'll have written up on the front of the house 'Justine Duval lives here', like Whistler and all the other celebs who've lived in Cheyne Walk.

Somehow, you've got to find a way of making simply pots and pots of money with the minimum of effort, so that you can buy absolutely stunning clothes that even people like the stuck-up preppy Sixth Formers who don't acknowledge you exist would kill for.

And you've got to make a serious effort to be painfully beautiful, even if it means you have to live on vegetables, like Garbo. (As a first gesture I'll consider flossing between my teeth every night.)

You've got to promise, when you fall in love, it'll be with someone stunningly attractive and you'll not simply settle for just anyone, like Mummy did.

But most important of all — I want you to swear, whatever happens, you're not going to be anything like Jemima.

Don't let me down.

    Justine Duval

(I folded the page and stuffed it into an envelope, sealed it and wrote on the outside.)

Justine Duval:
NOT TO BE OPENED UNTIL AFTER 2000 AD

Then I wondered where on earth to put it, safe enough not to be discovered, memorable enough not to be forgotten. First of all I rolled it up and put it in a Grolsch bottle I had been saving as a memento of a party, and corked it tight. Then I hid the bottle on the top of the wardrobe. I considered for a moment the likelihood of this being undisturbed for the requisite number of years and decided it wasn't very likely at all. Then I wondered about throwing it into the Thames and trusting on someone eventually finding the bottle and sending the note back—this was even less likely. In the end I took the bottle and buried it at the end of the garden.

I felt a real mal-co doing it, but afterwards I was seriously pleased with myself, if not mildly euphoric. I tried to picture that future me rediscovering it. The bottle with the envelope in it would come bobbing up over the years, riding time, with its message intact from today's Justine, marooned here in the present, to that mysterious unknown Justine of the future.

I made my way back into the house thinking deep fundamental thoughts about the meaning of life . . . whether it has a purpose . . . or whether having an un-cool star sign can really cramp your style . . .

My father says the most important thing in life is to work hard at school—and manage your bank account without getting overdrawn. These two things achieved, everything else will apparently miraculously fall into place.

Actually, my father couldn't be more wrong. People who work hard at school invariably get spots or overweight, or both. And people who stay in credit are generally considered unsociably tight-fisted.

My mother seems to think that success comes to those who look presentable: '*It is possible to be smartly casual, Justine.*' She believes the key to instant popularity is to walk straight from the hips and to keep your hair out of your eyes . . . and to be nice to practically everyone. What my mother simply doesn't understand is that popularity isn't a matter of being nice to people, it's a matter of people being nice to you.

My sister, Jemima, has a more realistic view of life. She has found out that what actually counts is to have legs up to your armpits, be lean as a French bean and to have enough invitations to go all the way round your bedroom mirror. Only then can you afford to do well at school (or be nice to people for that matter). That's as long as you don't appear to work, of course. The merest hint of swotting is guaranteed social suicide.

So much for philosophy. Back to the harsh reality of the present. On returning to the house, I settled down in our personal, private sitting room. It used to be the playroom but Jemima covered up the Winnie-the-Pooh frieze with pictures she tore out of a Katharine Hamnett catalogue. (Tigger's tail is still visible—a small, comforting, striped reminder of our youth, appearing at regular intervals around the room.) I switched on the television, stretched out full length on the sofa and tried to feel Friday-ish. After simply ages it occurred to me what was so emphatically wrong—the phone hadn't rung for a good half hour. This was seriously tragic! I had my weekend social diary to fill. I hauled the telephone over to the sofa in order to remedy the situation.

My third call found someone in.

'Three-five-eight-four-three-double-chew-hello.'

It was the voice of Jason (Franz's half brother). Jason's got to the designer-stubble age and really fancies he's stud-rated. He likes to throw his weight around with Franz's friends. I wasn't going to give him the satisfaction of recognising his voice. So I simply said:

'Is Franz in?'

There was a slight pause while Jason relocated the Hollywood in his mouth.

'Sure thing, who's calling?'

'Justine.'

'Oh, right.' He didn't have to sound so obviously disappointed.

There followed a lot of distant shouting. Eventually the

wait was rewarded by Franz's familiar scream.

'Baby! Have you recovered from the sunbed blues?'

'Oh that. Forget it. What's all that noise?'

'Only the taps running. I'm in the bath with the portable. Hey, did you know that the hot and the cold sound different?'

'Rubbish.'

'They do, honestly. Just you listen.'

Mid-way through the experiment, I interrupted.

'Hold on a minute.'

'What is it?'

'Sebastian Symington-Smythe's just come out of his house.'

'Who's he, for God's sake?'

Sebastian Symington-Smythe is a boy who's lived in our street for as long as I can remember. I had been vaguely aware of him last summer riding up and down on his mountain bike. But, boy, they must have been putting something into his school dinners over the past term or so.

'Quel mega-hunk. He's all dressed for tennis. Baby, you should see those golden tanned hairy legs.'

'But who is he?'

'He's lived down the road for yonks but he used to be away at boarding school. I think he's been given the boot, but no-one will say why—it must be for something really dire. Mummy positively oozes hostility every time she sets eyes on him.'

'It'll either be drugs or homosexuality,' said Franz knowledgeably.

I peered through the curtains savouring the last heart-wrenching glimpse of Sebastian's receding form as he turned the corner towards the tennis courts.

'He looks pretty straight to me.'

'You can't always tell,' said Franz darkly.

'What if it's drugs. He might be battling against some terrible addiction.' I resolved to add him to my list of people to
pray for.

'Either way, Baby, no French kissing, he's probably got
Aids,' said Franz.

'You can't catch it from kissing, dumbo. Anyway, he
looks incredibly healthy to me.'

'They do, for years and years, and then it hits them. It says
so in the ads.'

'With friends like you, Franz, no-one's going to die of
ignorance. Why don't you drop by tonight and check him
over?'

'Can't. Daddy's in town and he's going to take me out for
a meal somewhere swanky.'

'Lucky you.'

'Yes, but I've half a mind to order a side salad and ask for
the money instead. I still owe Henry for that Kenzo suit she
couldn't squeeze her backside into.'

'Bet your father will bale you out if you ask him. Baby,
you don't know how lucky you are to have a father like that.
You have no idea how tight mine is.'

There was a muffled scream.

'Hey, I nearly dropped the phone. Do you think you get
electrocuted if you drop a portable in the bath?'

'Don't know, but I never dare wear my Walkman, just in
case.'

'How much do you bet me I won't do it?'

'A fiver?'

'Listen Justine, at this very moment you could be absolutely the last person to speak to me alive.'

'Franz, don't.'

The phone went dead.

'Three-five-eight-four-three-double-chew-hello.' The
voice was oily with charm.

'Jason.'

'Oh, it's you again,' he said flatly.

'I think Franz has just done herself in with a portable phone.'

'Sounds a novel way to go.'

'Do you think you could see if she's all right?'

There was more distant shouting up the stairwell.

'She says she'll call you tomorrow. Now do you think you two could stop hogging the phone, I'm expecting a very important call.'

I put down the phone and gazed at the television hoping to be entertained. The late afternoon sun reflected back off the screen. After switching channels umpteen times, I came up with what looked like the kind of suspense movie that demanded concentration, so I drew the curtains, turned up the volume and settled down to dial Henrietta's number.

'Hi, Henry. Looks like you might get the akkers for the Kenzo suit. Daddy mega-bucks is back in town.'

'How do you know?'

'Just spoke to Franz, he's taking her out for a slap-up tonight.'

'Some people get all the luck.'

'Her parents are so generous.'

'Well you know why, don't you?'

'No, why? Tell me.'

'Because they're divorced, stupid,' said Henry with the voice of experience.

'What difference does that make?'

Henry delivered the following facts with the level tone of one who has read the book, seen the movie, bought the T-shirt—in short, is stating the blindingly obvious:

'It's simple. When your parents get divorced you can just kind of play one off against the other. Each is scared rigid they're going to be seen as the stingy one. You only have to exaggerate a tincy-wincy bit about what one of them has given you and the other one is falling over themself to match it. It helps, of course, if they don't communicate.'

'My parents look as if they are all set to stay monotonously married for ever,' I said resignedly.

'Tough. However, look on the bright side.'

'What's that?'

'No step-brothers and sisters to mess up your room.'

With that piece of wisdom she hung up.

Possibly because of my involvement in the conversation, possibly because of the decibels emitted by the television, I hadn't heard the key turn in the front door lock.

A lightning glimpse of pinstripes and briefcase momentarily eclipsed the television screen.

'Justine,' exclaimed my father as he extricated himself from the telephone cable.

I dutifully turned the sound down with the remote control.

'Justine,' he started again, as he flung open the curtains. 'What I can't understand is why you have to sit in the dark when it's broad daylight?'

As the cold light of day flooded into the room, the scene of controlled disarray came to light. He gazed in disgust at the comforting collection of lipstick-stained teacups, half-full glasses of Coke, school bag, biker jacket, Travel Foxes, Edina Ronay cardie, Walkman, cassettes and assorted magazines with which I liked to surround myself, in order to block out the hideous barrenness of my life.

'Hello Daddy. Give us a smacker.'

'Feet off the sofa,' commanded my father, offering a rough cheek.

'Had a good day?' I asked with interest.

'And tidy up a bit, can't you,' he replied without conviction.

I leaned off the sofa and stacked one cassette on top of

another. This gesture of intent seemed to satisfy him and he headed off in search of his slippers and G-and-T.

That maddening sunlight was reflecting off the dust on the screen again. I pulled the curtains to a close so that the room resumed its comforting gloom and once more flopped down in front of the TV. I'd missed the gory bit of the suspense movie. But after switching channels for some minutes, I found the credits coming up on 'Home and Away'—the antipodian alternative I secretly preferred. Could I be permitted the time to give it my full attention? No such luck. I was interrupted by a hysterical ringing on the front doorbell.

The view through the spyhole revealed Jemima.

Even distorted by its enlarging glass, Jemima was disgustingly good-looking. With nature's callous disregard for fairness, it had given her the high cheekbones, the perfect nose and a fall of silky natural blonde hair that she had done absolutely nothing to deserve. Standing there on the doorstep, hot and cross from the rush-hour Tube, she looked only mildly and flatteringly flushed.

Jemima must have known I was looking because she put her tongue out and grimaced at the spyhole. Then she leant on the bell again.

Her entrance coincided with our father's lightning flight down the stairs.

'What on earth's going on?' he roared just as Jemima stormed in.

'Why the hell can't you open the door, Bratfeatures?' she addressed me with sisterly affection.

Jemima was clasping a bursting bag of school files, a bunch of roses, *Vogue, Blitz* and a squashed swiss roll.

'And who are the roses from?' I enquired.

'Me, actually,' replied Jemima with dignity.

'How much were they?' demanded Father.

'Special offer, two quid,' said Jemima.

And so the fireworks started.

'I don't give you an allowance to squander on flowers . . . And incidentally . . .'

Jemima swept past and threw herself down in my place in front of the television.

'Yes, Daddy?' She eyed him with her practised 'beguiling' gaze.

'Next time you borrow my D J without asking me, could you refrain from dousing it in Chanel?'

'Yes, Daddy.'

'And it's about time you tidied this place up a bit . . . look at it.'

At which point our mother appeared in the doorway.

'Would you like a nice cup of tea, darling?' she asked Jemima, and then paused, vaguely aware that something-was-going-on.

'No she would not like a nice cup of tea. If she wants tea, nice or stewed, she can get it herself. Look at the mess . . .' he continued.

It took a good half hour before I regained my seat in front of the television. By that time the sound of bath water and loud music from upstairs indicated that Jemima had started her evening ritual. The scent of bubble bath was wafting down the stairs.

The last rumblings of the storm could be heard at intervals from the kitchen.

'. . . And it wasn't just the flowers . . .'

'No, dear,' I heard my mother agree.

'It was flowers and magazines, *and* a swiss roll.'

'Well it could be worse, you know. Imagine what she could be buying at her age.'

The kitchen door closed.

I imagined.

Peace reigned. The smell of bubble bath was soothingly

familiar. *My* bubble bath, I realized. By the time I reached the landing I had discovered that Jemima also had *my* new bathrobe, *my* Walkman and *my* new Rap tape, AND *my* brand new pristine copy of *Just Seventeen*.

After a minute or two of fruitless shouting at the locked bathroom door, I went into her room casting round for suitable ammunition for a counter-attack. Her shoulder bag was lying on the bed. It yielded a few gems. I doused myself liberally with her Coco, lit up a Gitane *filtre* and put on her House tape, full volume.

On inaudible slippers, my father entered the room and mouthed at me furiously. Then he turned off the tape. He wouldn't calm down enough for me to explain that Jemima had started it all. And I wasn't actually smoking the cigarette, I had just lit it to irritate her. So I simply weathered the tirade and then made my way back downstairs vowing that when I grew up, if not long before, I was going to find some dark and irrevocable way of wreaking revenge on Jemima.

I sat on the sofa fuming, all hope of feeling Friday-ish had by now well and truly been abandoned.

It was an hour or two later that this most seriously mega-bizarre thing happened. As I mentioned earlier, I'd been a trifle concerned about my ultimate destiny. But this was something so out of the blue, so drastic, it was to change the course of my entire social life, my entire sex life and all the boring bits of life in between . . .

2

You're not going to believe this, but what happened was . . . I was sitting watching television. It was a pretty bad night—nothing but low-budget chat shows and documentaries about the Middle East—when the television started playing up. First of all there was a lot of white fuzzy interference and then a picture of this woman kept appearing. I tried changing channels but it didn't make any difference. No sooner had I switched to another programme than the same thing happened.

I was just getting desperate and about to phone Radio Rentals when 'this woman' looked straight through the screen at me and said:

'Justine? . . .'

As you can imagine, I nearly slid off the sofa with shock.

'Justine . . . are you there?' She shaded her eyes and peered out of the screen.

'Yes . . .' I tried to say. It came out as a sort of croak.

She appeared to hear my attempt at a reply!

'Thank God for that. I've spent hours trying to get through.'

I stared at the screen in disbelief. My tummy did a sort of double-somersault. I was rapidly coming to the conclusion that I had gone totally bonkers. Too much time on the sunbed perhaps . . . Could one get sunbed stroke? But I'd only had forty minutes . . . Maybe it was sauna stroke . . .

'Are you still there?'

'Yes,' I said automatically, without thinking.

What a fool I felt talking . . . *talking!* . . . to a television screen!

'Don't you know who I am?'

'I'm sorry,' I said. 'I've no idea. What on earth is going on?'

'Come on. Have a wild guess,' she said.

I stared at the screen. I hadn't the faintest idea. This woman looked in a way a bit like Jemima, but fatter, more made up, aged probably in her mid-twenties.

'Are we related in some way?' I asked guardedly.

Her clothes, for instance, were nothing anyone in our family would ever dream of wearing—a tight red body-suit that looked like something out of a third-rate James Bond movie. She was holding a weird kind of matt steel box thing. I couldn't get a very clear view, but it appeared to have some sort of screen surrounded by buttons and dials like an outsize calculator.

Beside it was a battered pack of cigarettes. She leant over and helped herself to one. That was when I noticed the scar on the inside of her right wrist. That was odd, because I had a scar in exactly the same place, where I had burnt myself on Jemima's curling tongs.

'You're not going to believe this . . .' she said, taking a deep drag on her cigarette and eyeing me critically.

'Believe what?' I said with a sinking feeling.

'Well, as a matter of fact, I'm you.'

'What do you mean. You're me?'

The woman took another drag.

'You wrote to me, didn't you?'

'You're trying to say you're me, but . . . somehow . . . in the future?' I said slowly. My hands were starting to get that cold clammy feel—like wildly unattractive boys get when they're trying to hold hands in the cinema. This was really freaking me out!

'Well, there's no need to look so amazed,' she said as if her sudden appearance was the most normal occurrence in the world.

'But I don't understand . . .'

'I kind of thought you wanted me to get in touch.' She took another drag on her cigarette and stared at me with her uncomfortably assessing eyes.

'Well yes, no . . . I don't know. I mean, I didn't expect you to turn up, like this, on *television*! How on earth did you do it?'

'Don't ask! It took hours to get through. Not to mention the yonks it took to sort out the tracking.'

'This is really creepy,' I said.

'Why creepy? You study Physics, don't you?'

'Yes, but I'm not exactly brilliant at it.'

'Well, at least you must be aware that time is, what-do-you-call-it, "relative" . . . It's just a matter of re-programming, that's all.'

'So why isn't the whole world over-run with people dropping in on themselves?'

'It is.'

'It is?'

'You know that fuzzy kind of electronic buzzy stuff you get between programmes?'

'Static?'

'That's just it. It isn't static. It's people trying to get through. But they've been censored—jammed out.'

'What do you mean—jammed out? Why?'

'Look, just use your head. Think of the implications! I

mean, before the regulations came in there was this guy who got hold of all the old file copies of that pink Financial Thingummy . . .'

'The *Financial Times*?'

'Ummm. Anyway, apparently he just kept feeding himself the figures on all the shares that went up.'

'He must have made an absolute bomb!'

'He did. But he kept it all to himself. No-one knew a thing about it until one morning his wife woke up to find that he simply dematerialized. There he was at seven a.m., sitting up ready for his morning cuppa from the Teasmade. Next thing she knew, she was passing the cup to an empty pair of pyjamas. Seems his future life had simply taken over. It took them two months to track him down to this vast mansion on the Costa Brava . . . Marble floors throughout and two swimming pools . . .'

'Safe!'

'Yep, he had three girlfriends living in by then. It was all over the papers . . . Took years to sort out the divorce.'

'So why aren't you . . . er . . . *jammed out?*'

'Well, it just so happens that I've got this friend who's a bit of a Com-Tec freak. You know, Com-mun-i-ca-tions-Tech-nology?' She spelt it out as if I were a moron or something.

'Oh yes . . .'

'Well, he designs the programs for all that kind of stuff, so naturally he's a bit of a whizz at debugging it . . .'

She leant forward. 'The thing is,' she added in a conspiratorial tone, 'it's not exactly legal so we've got to keep this to ourselves or we're going to be in deep you-know-what.'

'Of course,' I said. Actually, I couldn't exactly picture myself trying to explain this sort of thing to anyone anyway.

'And you'd better be careful to do exactly as I say because, frankly, I don't fancy waking up one day in an empty pair of pyjamas.'

'Absolutely . . . you can count on me . . .' I said.

'God, the picture quality is so unspeakably dire,' she interrupted.

She jabbed at a button on the box with one of her puce-coloured nails. 'Now I can see you all right, Jeesus, I'd forgotten what a mess my hair used to be. Can you see me OK?'

'Well, you're a bit fuzzy round the edges.'

At that point she started to fade out.

'Justine . . .' I called.

She banged the top of the box and the picture came clearer again.

'That better? And don't call me Justine by the way. Call me Juste.'

'Juste?'

'Umm, I think it suits me better. Don't you?'

One thing I'd always secretly wanted was a nickname—'Juste' had just never seemed to have occurred to anyone. It sounded pretty cool . . .

Juste continued without giving me time to respond: 'Actually, your letter made me think . . . There are quite a few things I'd like to change about me . . . Actually, in fact, about you.'

'(What a cheek!)'

'Such as?' I enquired.

'Oh I don't know. It's just that life might have turned out better if I'd done things differently, that's all.'

'You mean, you're not brilliantly successful . . .'

'Not exactly,' she said defensively. 'But I'm working on it.'

Now this wasn't simply like being told you've got a D-minus-minus in a History essay, this was my whole future she was talking about. And she sounded so *resigned* about it.

'Well, I suppose it's not the end of the world,' I said, trying to hide a panic attack under a suitably objective and sympathetic front. 'As long as you're good at something.'

'Frankly, I've made rather a mess of things,' said Juste.

My heart sank another couple of kilometres. This conversation was not turning out at all the way I liked. I was just about to enquire into the nature of this 'mess' when she went on speaking forcefully: 'The thing is, your letter made me realize, it's never too late . . . Basically, it's up to you to do things differently.'

'What do you mean?'

'Well, for a start, couldn't you be a teensy bit more adventurous, break out a little? You don't have to be such a mouse.'

'What do you mean, a "mouse"?' I felt deeply insulted.

'Well, you could get something done to your hair.'

'I like it like this,' I said, sweeping it back out of my eyes.

'Suit yourself,' she said. 'But your clothes . . .' She stared pointedly at my ripped jeans. 'You do get a clothes allowance, don't you?'

I nodded.

'Well, if I were you—which I am as it happens—I'd spend it on something fit to be seen in.'

'Really?'

'Really! . . . Anyway,' she continued, 'there may be one or two little things we could agree on to make the future a little rosier for both of us. So I'll keep in touch.'

'You mean you can just sort of pop up on the screen whenever you feel like it?'

'Well, this is the twenty-first century, darling—at least for me it is. As you can imagine, things have moved on a bit.'

And with that she disappeared from the screen in a kind of electronic fizz.

I was left stunned, staring at the television in amazement.

19

Had what I thought had just happened, just happened?

I clicked through the channels but the normal selection of Friday night programmes appeared in the normal way.

Maybe I'd just imagined it . . . or been the victim of some unlikely and elaborate hoax. I sat there half expecting someone to waltz through the door with a microphone congratulating me, between bouts of convulsive sniggering, for being 'game for a laugh'.

No-one did. I walked to the window and drew back the curtains. The world outside looked reassuringly ordinary. I mean, was it so impossible? If you're potty enough to write to yourself in the future, your future self could well turn out to be crazy enough to want to get back to you. Would technology make such a mammoth leap forward? Surely such things could become possible?

But to see yourself . . . in the future . . . in the flesh . . . !

Actually I was a bit horrified to see quite how I'd turned out.

3

The next morning, Saturday, I woke up wondering if I'd actually dreamt all this. The more I puzzled over it, the more puzzled I felt. So I decided to dismiss the whole thing from my mind and see if it happened again.

In the meantime, Saturday required the ritual meeting of 'The Pack' in the King's Road. 'The Pack' is a whole group of us from Fourth Form; the name comes from Jemima christening us years ago, the 'Brat Pack' after the movies. We dropped the Brat part for obvious reasons but 'The Pack' stuck because it sounded fairly cool. The Saturday meeting was pretty crucial because that was when word went around about who was laying on the entertainment and where. It was a way of ensuring that any party had the requisite number of would-be gatecrashers outside to show it wasn't a flop. Anyway, that's where I was going on the top of a Number 22.

The bus toiled slowly up the King's Road. From my vantage point up in front, I could observe the display of talent. I recognised a few of the pairs of regulation well-faded US 501 originals and noted whose arm happened to be around whom that particular morning.

There was the usual drift of Casuals up from the country in

their trainers and T-shirts with messages on them—easy prey for the boys and girls giving out free hair-consultation leaflets. We passed the Dôme with its crowd of thirty-year-olds chatting up world-weary eighteen-year-olds. And the Chelsea Potter with its sixty-year-olds chatting up even wearier twenty-year-olds of assorted sexes and colours.

At last I spotted a small, familiar, disorderly group outside Gossips and jumped off between stops to join them.

'Isn't anyone going in for a drink?'

'We've been thrown out twice, so we thought we'd move on,' said Max.

Gossips kind of tolerated our crowd early on when they weren't too full but remembered the over-eighteen rule when they got busy later in the day. The group broke into twos and threes and we sauntered on up towards Sloane Square.

Dodging neatly-dressed Chelsea ladies, Saturday morning Sloanes in their Barbours heading for the General Trading Company and the occasional stray punk who hadn't been told that whole scene was over, we were approaching Peter Jones. Franz was giving a graphic account of the last time her mother took her shopping in this despised shop.

'It was a deep shade of yuk and that sort of no-man's-length between mini and middle-aged, and the shop-assistant was ganging up with my mother, telling me how wonderful I looked . . .'

'Hi there . . .'

A small orchestra of violins played, angels danced on pink clouds above our heads, the King's Road kind of bounced up, then gently regained its usual level, as I gazed into a pair of deep green eyes randomly and delectably flecked with hazel.

'Hello,' I managed to reply, praying that the pavement would dissolve beneath my feet or a jumbo jet land on my head—anything to distract him from the blush that was spreading up my neck and over my face.

'Would you like a free hair consultation?'

'Why not?'

I took the handout he offered.

After this epic exchange of wit, I moved on.

'That was Him,' I stage-whispered to Franz.

'Who?'

'You know, Sebastian S-S, the one I told you about.'

'But he's horny.'

'Oh, He's not bad,' I said modestly.

'What's he doing giving out Snippers handouts?'

'Guess He's trying to make some extra cash.'

'And you say he lives in your street?'

After that my rating went up about fifty points. Leonie (Miss Popularity 1991) even suggested treating me to a hot chocolate in Oriel.

There was the usual jockeying for position, but eventually we were all seated at a passably good table in the window. Franz was in her favourite place facing out towards the street so that she could get the best view of the display of talent around the Monument. (Franz's taste in males could be described as 'catholic' and I'm not referring to religion here — virtually anything that's potentially into shaving will do.) Max (the current Form Four Agony Aunt) was beside her ready to make impressed or sympathetic noises as appropriate when Franz poured out the latest on her love life. Henry, who is generally our organisational genius, was positioned facing inwards — she's developed this minor thing about the new half-French waiter with the ponytail and wanted to establish eye contact. Leonie was in the prime position centre-table in full view of both the window and the waiters, and I was in the favoured position beside her.

We had ordered three hot chocolates and three slices of chocolate gateau between five of us and were trying to kind of surreptitiously share when I realized I was still clasping the

Snippers handout.

'Are you going to go for this free consultation thing then?'

'I might.'

There was a verbal scuffle over who should accompany me.

Predictably, Leonie won. Leonie should actually have been in Fifth Form but she had descended to our level for some academic reason that was shrouded in deepest mystery. Rumours had been rife about her IQ level, but I put more faith in the authorised version—that the demands of her social life had just ruled out the possibility of homework. Fate had smiled on Leonie and she had grown early: by fifteen she had the height and poise (and ability to hold a Gitane *filtre* without looking ostentatious) of a seventeen-year-old. Inevitably she favoured the older man, boys of eighteen and above—especially if they were sun-bronzed, green-eyed and prone to hanging around the King's Road, giving out Snippers handouts.

I suppose she had some sort of impression that Sebastian might happen to be there, inside the salon.

He wasn't.

Instead, we were greeted by a receptionist called Nigel who handed us over to a hair stylist called 'Shea'.

'Would you like to come through?'

We followed Shea as she writhed her way across the salon in a minimal black body-clinging dress which barely met a pair of fishnet tights before they were swallowed by her high-heeled patent boots.

She hovered behind my chair, shifting painfully from boot to boot, fingering my hair with professional distaste.

'This is your natural colour, isn't it?'

'Yes,' I admitted with shame.

'Of course, you do have a tendency to scurf, I wouldn't like to call it dandruff. Our tricologist calls every Tuesday evening. I could arrange an appointment for you.'

I should have recognised this as part of the demoralisation process prior to brain washing.

'And where did you last have it cut?'

I simply couldn't own up that Henry usually cut it for me.

'Spain,' I said, with sudden inspiration.

'That's nice,' said Shea. Now on familiar territory she was warming to me. 'I went to Majorca last year, incredible night-life . . .' she paused. 'Still, I suppose you're not into that sort of thing yet, are you?'

I raised myself to my full height in the chair.

'I was wondering if I ought to have highlights,' I said with dignity.

At the mention of this magic word she produced a colour chart with a flourish. Apparently, one didn't just highlight any more. One highlighted and lowlighted, choosing a number—a minimum of three—of different shades to give the whole head a *natural* effect.

Leonie poured over the colour chart. The two of them were having a high old time choosing the right combination. I looked on helplessly, wondering how much it would all cost.

Shea tottered off to mix the colours.

That was when I heard the echo of a voice in my mind—Juste's voice.

'Mouse!'

I looked in the mirror. It was true I had mousey clothes, mousey hair. It was no wonder I hadn't had a passionate affair yet. Or even a more than one-date relationship.

'You think I ought to have the highlights then?' I asked Leonie.

'You only live once,' she said.

'But it's going to cost a fortune.'

'It's an *investment*, darling,' said Leonie in a world-weary voice. 'You don't want to be a social dropout, do you? Anyone can "suffer for beauty" but you "pay for success".'

'How much do you think this will all cost?' I whispered.

Leonie pointed out that I was getting a ten per cent reduction with the handout anyway.

'And think what you're saving on magazines. You can read this month's *Harpers*, *Vogue* and *Tatler* for absolutely nothing.'

'Big deal.'

By the time Shea reappeared I had decided that even if I found out what the damage was going to be, it wasn't worth the humiliation of walking out.

For a good three quarters of an hour I sat pinioned to the seat looking like a Walt Disney vulture as Shea completed the task of dragging my hair through a kind of perforated bathing cap.

I have a sensitive scalp and a very low pain threshold. In fact, I'm the only one in the class who hasn't defied their parents and had their ears pierced. And it's not because I'm a failure as a rebel—I'm just a total physical coward. Anyway, one positive thing came out of the experience, it was the very last time I was having my hair highlighted.

Leonie and I had looked at all the magazines and caught up on who wasn't in *Tatler* this month. Any hope of seeing Sebastian had long since faded. So she announced that she might as well be off.

I was left to study the interior decor—a combination of dusty black walls, ailing palms and neo-Sixties chrome and plastic. When no-one was around, I indulged in furtive bouts of reading the seedier bits of *Cosmopolitan*'s problem page. *Quel* education, it was enough to put you off sex for life!

As Shea combed through my damp and now multi-coloured hair, she announced, 'I'm going to have to cut it, you know. It's all over the place,' and she muttered libellous things about foreign hairdressers.

I had thirty pounds in my purse provided by my mother for the purpose of buying a new pair of jeans for school. My last ones had mysteriously developed designer rips over the holidays. But then again, I also had all the money the others had given me to pay my mother back for the tickets she'd bought for the Blue Ribbon Ball—which we'd attended to aid one of her favourite causes. (We'd all agreed at the time that this was to be our very last Charity Teenage Ball.)

I thought of Juste. What had she done to nurture those savage cascades of waves? How dare she call me a mouse.

'Go ahead,' I said. 'Cut it.'

'I'll just give it a trim,' she said.

Unfortunately, Shea hadn't been told that nobody—but nobody—has their hair layered these days. After all, how can one seductively sweep the hair out of one's eyes if one doesn't have the hair to flop seductively into them?

Two and a half hours and *fifty five pounds* later I stood fuming in the King's Road. The Chelsea ladies were still making their way into Peter Jones. The Sloanes were still striding towards the General Trading Company. The punks still posed for the ever-mutating group of tourists. The world continued to revolve with callous indifference to my own personal misery.

'It's really not at all bad from the back,' said Max as I tucked into a late, late burger at Ed's Diner. 'How much was it?'

'It would be kinder not to ask.'

That was when the 'Mafia' turned up. The 'Mafia' is the name the Pack has given to the group of people who currently run the London Social Scene—organising Black Tie balls, Energy parties and that kind of thing. They tend to frequent Ed's late on Saturday. They drive up in classy cars which they park ostentatiously outside on the double yellow line, so that they have to keep getting up and checking for wardens and drawing attention to them. They mostly wear Ray-Bans even when it rains and usually come accompanied by a number of pin-thin girls who they balance on bar stools to show off their legs. And they never drink anything stronger than Perrier water.

Max and I sat around a bit longer feeling self-conscious. But it soon became clear that all they were after were our bar stools within view of the window, so we left.

It wasn't until back home that evening, after a lightning dash up the stairs to my room, where even my second back-up piggy bank failed to yield any cash, that the seriously dire nature of my financial situation hit me.

I sometimes fantasize about being an orphan. I realize that this must sound pretty cold and heartless and I'm really fond of my parents in spite of their many failings. But just imagine a world without parents. All the money they uselessly hoard away in shares and property and investment accounts could be released by benevolent trustees and channelled towards the things that really matter.

I stared miserably out of the window at the neat rows of dahlias tied and staked like so many prisoners awaiting execution. It was the orderliness of adult life that was so tedious. And how they try to inflict it on you . . . proper bed-times, regular meals and miserly amounts of money, drip-fed through in an allowance.

At length, I decided to confide in Jemima; you never knew—it might just have been one of her good days.

I penetrated into the James Dean Memorial Sanctuary.

Jemima was busy arranging a new bunch of flowers in her window.

'You know those will only wither if you leave them in the

sun,' I said.

She ignored this and started being scathing about my hair-style.

'Sad case,' she said. 'Still, you never know, white stilettos might make a comeback — anything could happen.'

When I explained about the financial crisis, she agreed that it was 'seriously tragic', and suggested I found a Saturday job. Then she started doing her eye make-up. So much for sisterly advice.

Henry was more help on the phone.

'So if you were only going to buy a pair of secondhand 501s anyway, you can have the ones I've out-grown. Just run an iron over them and stick them in an American Classics carrier. Your mother will never know the difference.'

'But what about the Ball ticket money?'

'Easy. You can just keep stalling her by saying none of us would pay up.'

'Henry, you're a genius.'

Of course, it didn't alter the dire nature of the haircut. I had wet it, backcombed it and rubbed gel into it and I was almost coming to terms with the fact that I might one day be able to face the outside world when ... IT HAPPENED AGAIN!

Juste made an appearance just as I was in the middle of a con-soling session with one of Jemima's James Dean videos.

James Dean was just about to *almost* kiss Natalie Wood when Juste appeared in her place. She had matched herself in so it actually looked as if she was part of the film — it was bril-liant. However, believe it or not, she took no notice whatso-ever of James Dean and simply stared out of the screen and said: 'My God, what on earth have you done to your hair?'

'You just interrupted the very best bit!'

'No hassle, you can rewind! Answer my question!'

'Basically I had it done to please you . . .'

'Please me!'

'But it turned out to be a bit of a mistake.'

'I should say it did.'

James Dean by this time was slumped and despondent, putting on his hurt dog expression.

'Now listen to me,' said Juste. 'Are you concentrating?'

'Yes!'

'If you are willing to co-operate, you just might have a chance of the kind of rosy future you have in mind. If not . . .' she paused.

'If not?' I prompted.

'Well, you're just going to end up like me, aren't you?'

I nodded.

'So before doing anything rash . . . consult me next time, OK?'

'OK,' I said.

And she faded herself out.

I sat there for a minute feeling dazed. Then, coming to my senses, I realized there was a way to prove whether or not Juste had actually appeared.

Breathlessly, I rewound.

But when I played the tape back, Juste wasn't on it . . . Strange!

My parents didn't get a full-on confrontation with the haircut until drinks-before-dinner-time. My mother was furious about the highlighting but gave the cut the kiss of death by saying it looked 'tidier'.

My father just glanced up from the *Financial Times* and asked how much it had cost.

'Well, it will have to come out of your allowance,' he announced when I admitted to half the figure. And he continued to check his share prices. The callousness of parents!

4

I could hear my mother downstairs on the phone.

'Yes . . . Yes, speaking.'

There was a pause and then a total change of voice.

'Yes, Jemima. That's right. Umm, eighteen in April.'

She stood transfixed holding a pair of pinking shears in the air. Then, after a further pause, 'Well, I don't know. I'll have to ask her.'

'. . . Ummm . . . I imagine it would. Well, why don't you come round for a drink, you could talk it over with him too.'

There was ruffled consultation of her Filofax.

'Umm . . . Friday would be fine. Seven-thirty-ish?'

She put down the phone and turned to me, a little flushed.

'*Do you know who that was?*'

'No idea,' I said.

She stage whispered the name of a well-known society figure.

'Who's he?'

'He wanted to know if Jemima is coming out this year.'

'Coming out of what?'

But my mother wasn't listening. She was bustling up the stairs waving the pinking shears.

'Jemima . . . Jemmy . . . listen . . .'

I was intrigued, so I followed at a distance. As I reached the bedroom door I started to catch snatches of their conversation.

Mummy: 'Just think of all the people you'd meet.'

Jemima: 'I meet enough people as it is.'

Mummy: 'Yes, but what *sort* of people?'

Jemima (heating up): 'What do you mean, what *sort* of people.'

Mummy: 'Jemima, you know exactly what I mean.'

It all ended with:

'Frankly, Mummy, I wouldn't be seen dead as a Deb.'

My mother had to back down, defeated.

'Well . . .' she said and took a deep breath: 'Quite honestly, Jemima, I sometimes ask myself if all the money lavished on sending you to that school wasn't wasted. I know at first hand from Jane Ponsonby-Haugh that Fiona simply leapt at the idea. But you don't seem the least bit interested in social contacts. However, if that's how you feel, I suppose I'll simply have to put him off.'

'I suppose you will,' said Jemima as our mother disappeared downstairs. I heard her blowing her nose hard as she consoled herself with a catalogue on conservatories.

'The trouble with Mummy,' said Jemima, when she was sure she was out of earshot, 'is that she expects everyone to be like her. You know how she can't resist joining things. All this Deb business is because she's simply dying to get on the Berkeley Dress Show committee.'

I nodded in silent agreement, but I wondered deep down how Jemima could possibly want to miss all those parties.

Jemima was right, of course. Mummy was on countless committees. She was forever racing out to Fund-raising Meetings, or spending hours on the phone gathering support for the Prevention of Things. All through our lives we had suffered interminable tea parties and coffee mornings for

32

what we called the Tracksuit-and-Pearls set as they gathered at our house to cover padded coathangers in Liberty print or make lace-frilled Kleenex holders for their charity bazaars. We hadn't attended these gatherings, of course; our job had been to entertain the workers' offspring as they were thrust on us as bewildered and unwelcomed guests.

Her latest and most seriously-worrying endeavour, from my point of view, had taken place this month. Daddy had unintentionally implied over dinner that Mummy didn't take enough interest in our education.

'Nonsense,' she had replied. 'I always read their reports most thoroughly.' But she had retaliated by joining our school's Parent/Teacher Association.

This was bad news. For a start one likes to keep home life and school life nicely separated. If things get heavy at home one can always make out everything's fine at school and vice versa. The system is threatened enough by those dire parent/teacher evenings when they all get a chance to put their heads together. But to have a parent actually making unscheduled incursions into school territory is seriously worrying.

Jemima and I go to an all-girls' private day school. Actually, you couldn't really get a better preparation for the bitter realities of life. If you can survive the 'Mansard Hall' jungle, you can survive anything. Jemima's in Upper Sixth, so close to leaving she's switched off anyway. I'm in Fourth Form, so I'm in the thick of it.

The first thing to understand about this year's Mansard Fourth Form is the Power Structure. Currently, it goes something like this:

At the top you get the S S (Socially Successful), rated 80-90 out of 100. This is a small élite group which comprises Leonie (Miss Popularity 1991) and a couple of heavies (metaphor-ically-speaking) who hang around with her: Tom (Thoma-sina)—her father's a well-known actor, so she doesn't have to make much of an effort, and Go-go (Georgina) who's got a boyfriend and, rumour has it, has actually 'done it'—but I think that's probably an over-claim. These three keep very much to themselves, although they do condescend to mix sometimes with some girls of lower rating who have elder brothers (like Franz), especially if the brothers go somewhere like Eton or Stowe.

Next in the pecking order come a load of us like Franz, Henry, Max and myself, rated approximately 50-80 (these are my own calculations, so I may be being over-modest). We generally invest in the right labels, but we're not up in the 80s because none of us has yet established a more than two-week relationship with a male. In general, I think we are pretty happy in our mid-way position; we don't have the insecurity of being at the top and it's a big enough group to give us some flexibility.

Then there's the Non-Descripts, rated 30-50, the majority of the class, in fact. It is possible to rise from this group if you do something really noticeable (like appear in *Tatler*, or get a modelling assignment or, even better, your parents get a mention in Dempster's), but generally this group gives up the battle after a term or two and settles down in protective twos or threes who keep to themselves.

These are followed by the Dregs, lost causes rated 30 and below; these are people who either swot, or have clothes bought by Mummy from M&S or BHS, or are generally overweight or have acne or something. We are all very nice to them (which proves just how desperate their situation is). Very often, when you meet their parents you realize they can't help being socially handicapped, a lot of it is simply in the genes.

Anyway, as you can see, the Power Structure is quite straightforwardedly based on social success.

That's where the Parents' Committee comes in. If there's

one thing parents can't stand, it's the fact you have a social life. Instead of concerning themselves with innocent preoccupations like new-mothers'-coffee-mornings and fund-raising-drinks-parties, they've discovered this movement called Parent Power. I know because Mummy's got this little Gucci bag that's always bursting at the seams. It just happened to fall open after the last Parents' Meeting and a crushed photostat fell out headed: 'How to Handle the Young Adult'. Naturally, I realized it would be helpful if I cast a glance over it.

I got on the phone to Franz straight away.

'Listen, I'm telling you, this is serious.'

'This Parent What's-it, where on earth did they get the idea from?'

'Parent Power—apparently someone's imported it from the States. It's all because they're dead scared over there that they're breeding a nation of addicts or alcoholics or husband-swoppers.'

'Well, they are, aren't they? Look at "Dullarse'n'Dysentry", not to mention "Twin Tits". What's that got to do with us?'

'Apparently, someone has suggested that we're getting "out-of-hand".'

'We should be so lucky. Anyway, what's this Parent Power thingie going to do about it?'

'Sounds like a real crackdown on funds, curfew times etc . . . '

I straightened out the crumpled page. 'Oh boy, and Prohibition too. Listen to this, they want all the parents to sign a pledge that there will be strictly no alcohol served at parties.'

'So it's goodbye to the jolly cider-punch and watered-down Sangria. And back to the old vodka hip-flasks like in First Form.'

'And they even want our phone calls monitored.'

'Censorship too, this is serious, man.'

'According to my information source, the first meeting is scheduled for next Tuesday evening. They're going to show a video from the London Parents' Action Group.'

'Ser-i-ous. We've got to find some way of infiltrating. First rule of battle—decent counter-intelligence.'

I was silent for a moment, something had just occurred to me.

'Justine, are you still there?'

'Umm. You've given me an idea.'

'Like what?'

'I need time to work on it. I'll ring you later.'

I put the receiver down thoughtfully.

It was *still* bothering me. Was this Juste appearance thing a total figment of my imagination? The sure way to tell was to check it out with someone else. But then, can you imagine casually dropping into the conversation to anyone—even to your very best friend: 'By the way, would you say that's me on the television—in the future, of course?'

What was really frustrating was never knowing when she'd make an appearance. I started to keep up a vigil in front of the television. Mummy had obviously decided I was turning into a tele-freak and had begun to make dark hints about enrolling me into Badminton or Squash or Aerobics classes. Then, at last, Juste came through—maddeningly enough it would be just as 'Top of the Pops' was getting to Number One . . .

Extremely loud music was playing in the background and she had painted her eyes with thick lines in a series of bright clashing colours.

'Are you having a party or something?' I asked.

'Just got a few friends round.'

I was intrigued by the friends. What kind of friends would I have? I wondered.

'Who? What are they like?' I strained my ears trying to catch the sound of any voices.

Juste frowned and looked at me, she seemed about to say something and then she changed her mind.

'No-one you'd know,' she said.

'I do think you're being awfully cagey,' I said. 'You never actually tell me anything about yourself.'

'Honestly,' said Juste. 'Can you imagine what it would be like to grow up knowing exactly what was going to happen to you?'

I tried to imagine.

'It might make life a trifle predictable,' I suggested.

'Baby, believe me. It would be like knowing the punch-line before you've heard the joke,' said Juste. 'Life simply wouldn't be worth living. Incidentally, what are you doing with yourself? You're not going to spend your entire life lazing in front of the TV, are you?'

'Quite possibly. We've got a Parent Power crisis on our hands. If something isn't done about it TV may be about the wildest leisure activity on offer. These Power-crazed Parents are aiming to totally undermine our social credibility. No booze, no boys, no late nights and no late movies . . . It's social death, man. We've got to move fast or Mansard's Fourth Form could simply disappear from the London scene. Unless, that is, you could maybe put in a word or two on our behalf?'

'Tell me about it,' said Juste.

I gave her a brief rundown. Juste listened with a con-centrated frown, then said: 'If you're suggesting what I think you're suggesting—you want me to make an appearance at the Parents' Meeting?'

'Do you think you could do it?'

'Provided I had the precise time of the meeting, I think I could probably manage something in that line.'

'What could you do exactly?'

'Well, assuming I get through, I think I could slot myself into their video and when it came to an appropriate place I could put in a few well-chosen words.'

'You'd have to dress the part, of course,' I said.

'Don't worry. I'll pop into a Charity Shop and find something "Nineties".'

'Nothing too wild . . . and you might tone down the make-up.'

'Don't fret. I must say it will be rather fun to see the old place again.'

'So you'll do it?'

'It could be quite a laugh . . . as long as I don't get recognised of course.'

'I think that's highly unlikely,' I said. 'Seriously, can you imagine anyone in their wildest flights of fancy thinking that you are me?'

Juste looked at me, rather pityingly as it happens.

'Well no, perhaps not.'

'And if I can do anything for you in return . . . ?'

'You can, as a matter of fact,' said Juste.

'Like what?'

'Well, you can get your teeth straightened for a start. It drives me crazy the way this front side one overlaps. You know the one I mean?'

'But that means a brace for God-knows-how-long.'

'You'll regret it if you don't do it now,' said Juste.

'I'll think about it,' I conceded.

'And another thing. Can you stop making such a pig of yourself on the chocolate brownies. You've no idea what a struggle I've had keeping my weight down.'

'What makes you think I've been eating brownies?'

'I remember—remember?'

I turned off the television thinking that maybe, in actual fact, I wasn't turning out so badly after all. Plenty of loud music in the background—a few friends around—and she was willing to stand up for our rights against the Parents' Committee too. That couldn't be bad.

5

That Saturday night, Franz's Wrinklies had slid off to Glyndebourne or somewhere, so the gang was having a sleep-over at her house.

It was the usual scene: Franz over-microwaved the lasagne and we burnt a saucepan 'caramelizing' the popcorn. As a 'starter' we were all tucking into the only success of the night—The Mars Fridge Cake—when Max suggested:

'Perhaps we ought to have a glass of wine to kind of wash it down.'

We peered into Franz's stepfather's wine cellar.

'I know some of it's worth a fortune,' said Franz. 'How do we tell which is which?'

We studied the unfamiliar labels.

'I had some German wine last week which was really yummy,' said Max.

'Max darling, no-one, but no-one, drinks German wine, didn't you know?' said Henry.

'In that case they're crazy. Hey look, no problem, some of these bottles have got prices on. We can just pick a cheapo. Look, this one is only five-eighty and it's covered in dust.'

'We ought to have red anyway. With pasta,' said Franz.

'OK, know-all, so you open it.'

'This wine has a lot of alcohol in it,' said Henry, holding her glass up to the light.

'How do you know?'

'The alcohol test. You remember, in Biology. You can tell by the way it clings to the glass.'

'It tastes awfully strong, do you have any Coke?' asked Max.

'Only Diet Pepsi.'

'It'll have to do.'

We watched as Max mixed a glass, half-and-half wine and Pepsi. She passed it round.

'That's really good,' said Henry.

'OK chaps, cocktail time,' said Franz. She mixed a big jugful and added loads of ice.

After dinner we piled the dishes haphazardly into the dishwasher and settled down to watch the video.

'I'm afraid it's only a "Fifteen",' said Franz apologetically. 'I had to use my brother's video card. The guy in the shop lets me get away with the "Fifteens" but there's no way he'll let me take out an "Eighteen".'

It wasn't too bad though because it made Max feel sick. She's pretty susceptible to horror films. In fact on the Max-rating it was really good because she nearly actually threw up, unless it was that third jugful of cocktail, of course.

It was about 1 a.m. when we finished watching the video. By that time we all felt too psyched-up to sleep so Franz, being the real hostess, started reading the *Just Seventeen* Problem Page out loud to get us all sleepy. There was this letter from a fifteen-year-old who was really worried because she'd never been kissed.

'Hard case,' said Henry. 'Just imagine, maybe she's got ferocious breath or something.'

The others murmured agreement, but I didn't say much because, frankly, I hadn't much to boast about in that area.

Unless you count being kissed in the spaghetti game, of course.

'I remember the first time,' said Franz, dreamily.

'What was he like?' asked Max.

'He was really old. Almost eighteen. He was doing A Levels and everything. Looking back on it now I reckon he was a bit of a child molester.'

'How old were you?' asked Max.

'Nearly thirteen.'

'So what happened?' There was a hush in the room.

'Pass the cocktail,' said Franz, and she took a swig. 'It was all terribly D H Lawrence.' She paused for effect. 'It was on a railway bridge with a train going under.'

'Gosh,' said Henry. 'It doesn't sound very intimate. Couldn't everyone see and everything?'

'No, stupid. We were on top of the bridge and the train was going underneath.'

'So did the earth move?' said Henry with a giggle.

Franz threw a pillow at her:

'No, but the bridge shook. Actually I've always wondered since. I mean, I always find that kissing tastes kind of metallic. Do you think it has something to do with the train?'

'Imagine if you never ever enjoy it, and it's all that guy's fault,' said Max with a sigh. 'I mean, maybe you've been permanently psychologically warped by the experience.'

'Don't break your heart over it,' said Franz. 'I made up for it last year with my French exchange's cousin.'

'French kissing, eh?' said Henry.

'You could call it that. Anyway, who's next? I'm not going to be the only one to reveal my deep and darkest,' said Franz.

'Max is next,' said Henry.

'No, I couldn't.'

'Come on, fair's fair,' complained Franz. 'Just that first

incy-wincy peck.'

'OK. But you promise not to laugh.'

We all promised.

'We were both virtually starkers,' she said with effect.

'Max!'

'Yes, we were. It was at the swimming pool. Under water,' she added with a giggle.

'Gosh, *quel* pervert!' shrieked Henry. 'I bet I know who it was.'

'Who?'

'Dominic Thingummy.'

'How did you know?'

'He does it to all the girls. He nearly drowned me!'

'Henry's turn,' I called out, hoping desperately for some inspiration before it came to mine.

'Oh, awfully boring standard stuff really,' said Henry. 'My first ball. This boy came up and asked me to dance and I thought, "Why not?". Because he had quite a sexy haircut, although he was shorter than me. Well, only a bit. At any rate, it was a quick snog on the dance floor and then he disappeared to get me a drink and I never saw him again. I didn't even know his name. The only lasting impression I had was of his brand of cigarette smoke.

'What was it?' asked Max.

'Marlboro.'

'That sure singles him out from the crowd,' said Franz. 'If I bump into him, I'll tell him to write.'

'OK. Justine's turn.'

'The first?' I said. 'I'm not sure I can remember.'

'Oh, come on,' said Franz. 'Everyone can!'

I cleared my throat. I tried to imagine what Juste would say.

Automatically, I found myself saying:

'Well, it was no big deal really . . . It was one afternoon

when I was coming home from school and it was pouring with rain. Simply bucketing down. I was standing under a tree dripping wet, waiting for it to ease off a bit, when this boy came along who lives in our road.'

'Not the one with the sexy green come-to-bed eyes,' said Franz.

'There's no need to be so crude. But yes, as a matter of fact.'

'The one we all saw outside Snippers?'

'Uh huh.'

'He didn't exactly put on a repeat performance on Saturday,' said Franz—rather cruelly I thought.

'It's not that kind of relationship,' I countered.

'What sort of *relationship* is it then?' enquired Henry.

'Simply . . . utterly . . . poignant,' I said.

'Boy! . . .' said Max. 'Tell us about it.'

The room was so quiet you could have heard a Hermesetas drop.

'Well, He was carrying this big umbrella, and He held it out so as to shelter us both and said: "There's room for one more inside."'

'Yes . . .'

'He had to kind of put his arm around me while we walked along, you see, so we could keep in step. And when we got to the front door I turned around to say thank you and . . .' I paused for inspiration, '. . . He said, "You've got rain running down your neck", and bent down and kissed it.'

'What. Your neck?'

'Yes,' I said, feeling really embarrassed. 'Doesn't that count?'

'Definitely not,' said Franz.

'Rubbish,' said Henry. 'I think it's just about the sexiest thing I've heard in weeks.'

Fortunately, they got into a long and heated argument

over this, so the attention was taken off me.

The sleep-over didn't help the 'Getting-out-of-hand' situation. Firstly, Franz hadn't remembered to take the video out of the player. So her mother was treated to a dose of *Blood Brides of Vengeance* in place of her pre-programmed recording of a Conservative Party Political Broadcast.

And then there was the wine. According to Franz's step-father the 580 was francs not five-eighty sterling. (It was a Chateau Latour '81.) Henry was right about the alcohol, it was pretty strong. Curiously enough, it didn't seem to help when Franz told him we'd watered it down with Pepsi.

The timing was unfortunate too, because it provided more ammunition for the Parent Power meeting which took place at school the following Tuesday.

None of us attended, of course. I was aching to know what had happened but had to content myself with a sketchy second-person account from my mother.

'There was the most *extraordinary* woman on this video; I can't imagine what these schools are thinking of these days. Pass the mange-touts, Justine.'

Mummy tucked her napkin protectively into the top of her YSL blouse (she always likes to put on a good show at the school).

'What was she like?' I prompted.

'Well, she looked too young to know anything about bringing up teenagers. Very curiously dressed. I think that school is definitely going downhill.'

My father mumbled reassuringly about GCSE results.

'Exam results are all very well. But if the girls are becoming totally uncontrollable . . .'

I tried to remain expressionless.

'Well, we had all just about agreed about taking a firm

hand—yes Justine, there's no need to pull faces. But when they played the video on which *this woman* made these quite absurd suggestions—the meeting ended in a kind of uproar.'

'What sort of suggestions?' asked my father.

My mother raised an eyebrow and glanced over in my direction.

'I'll tell you after dinner.'

I got the low-down from Max, whose mother tells her everything. It was Juste all right. It seemed that she had suggested among other things: Total freedom of bed-times. The indefinite suspension of curfew times. Ashtrays to be fitted in desks. Walkmans to be on official equipment lists. Videos to be played in school libraries and video games in Computer Studies. And the next school fund-raising event to be something the girls could really relate to, like an Acid House party.

'And you've no idea what the woman was wearing,' ended Max.

'Tell me,' I said with foreboding.

Apparently, it had been a skin-tight punk mini-dress which sounded at least eight years out of date. What's more she was wearing it with a pair of Sixties kinky boots—and as if these weren't enough of an anachronism she had on a *vintage 1988 Swatch!*

'How did the Wrinklies react?'

'Noddy virtually got lynched.' (Noddy is our affectionate pseudonym for our beloved Head, mainly because her sidekick the bursar is extremely well-endowed ear-wise.)

'But what about the "funky lady"? Didn't anyone comment on her?'

'Well, I think most of the parents were so staggered they kind of drifted out of the meeting totally speechless, as if shell-shocked.'

'Poor dears,' I remarked sympathetically.

6

I had to give in, in the end, about having my teeth straightened. My mother had been going on at me for ages about
them, but when Juste joined in . . . She'd been cropping up a
lot lately, interrupting all my favourite programmes. What
really bugged me was the way she always managed somehow to bring the conversation round to teeth. Anyway I
guess that I owed her something for her Parent Power
appearance.

My mother insisted I went to a Harley Street orthodontist
so that I didn't miss school. Missing school was to have been
the only good thing about it!

The dentist spent a long time practically dislocating my
jaw before announcing the verdict.

'It'll mean a fixed brace, I'm afraid.'

My mother smiled comfortingly. She wasn't the one
whose sex life was about to become a non-option.

'How long for?'

The sentence was a year—*at least!*

A year! I'd be virtually past my 'Best before . . .' date by
the time it came off.

I was just about to object when he shoved a plate full of
pre-masticated chewing gum in my mouth.

'Just taking an impression.' He smiled as he held this in place with a vice-like grip. He had crooked teeth himself! I sat in the chair asking myself wasn't it life's little accidents and imperfections that make for true beauty? I started to list all the film stars I knew with crooked teeth. I didn't get past nought.

'They soon get used to it, you know,' he said to my mother as if I were a dog or something. 'No problem eating. They have to be careful about sweet things, of course.'

'I was wondering about her clarinet lessons,' said my mother, with a sudden fit of parental concern.

Every down side has a flip side.

The orthodontist paused and looked at me sympathetically.

'That could be difficult. I have heard of people getting round the problem by covering their brace with orange peel . . .'

My heart sank.

'. . . But I'm afraid you might have to give the clarinet a rest for a while.'

I did my best to look genuinely distressed.

'It's a pity about the clarinet, darling,' my mother said over a consoling tea in Liberty. 'But I'm sure Miss Bryce won't mind if you switch to piano for a term or two. And then in the spring Mr Hackett says you can have it off (my mother's choice of phrase was unfortunate, to say the least) and you need only wear a retainer at night.'

The actual instrument of torture (the brace, not the piano) was fitted two weeks later. By the time I reached home after the appointment I was painfully aware that the treatment was working. Jemima opened the front door for me.

'Hi Jaws, let's have a look? . . . God, that should keep you out of trouble. It must make quite a show when all the candles are lit.'

The worst thing about it, which I wouldn't admit to a soul, was that it meant I could no longer secretly suck my thumb. Another giant leap up the hard, rocky road to adulthood.

For some reason, and I had a sneaky suspicion that it might be because my fixed brace had removed me once and for all from the field of competition, Jemima had started to be nicer to me.

She was even nice to Chuck when he came round. Chuck's a boy I've known since I was born. In fact, technically speaking, since before. My mother met his mother at ante-natal classes at Queen Charlotte's. I don't think my mother and his mother would have got on at all if it hadn't been for the kind of intimacy engendered by lying flat out like beached whales doing breathing exercises together. It just so happened that his mother and my mother went into labour on the same day, so we're kind of unrelated twins. Chuck's father is a Maths teacher and they're not wildly rich or anything. I guess Chuck could get an assisted place in a private school but for some unfathomable political reason he goes to a comprehensive.

I was in the bath when he came round. Jemima came up to let me know.

'Prepare for a culture shock,' she said, putting her head round the door without knocking. 'CND's downstairs.' (Chuck's real name is Charles Nevil Davis. My father says that they must have done it on purpose.)

Anyway, by the time I got downstairs, I found Jemima talking to him quite amicably. She'd even found some apple juice for him. Chuck doesn't drink Coke on principle.

'Hey, you'll never guess what!' said Jemima. 'You really are twinnies now. Smile Chuck.'

Chuck smiled and revealed two rows of glinting metal.

After that, Jemima really spoilt her being-nice effort by going on about the couple who had to be carted off to hospital because they got their braces locked in a passionate embrace. I mean, there has never, absolutely never, been anything like that between Chuck and me, I swear. He's not even attractive, for God's sake.

'Anyway, watch it you two, you don't want to get metal fatigue,' said Jemima as a passing shot as she disappeared upstairs.

'New hairstyle,' said Chuck, when we were left together.

'Oh yes. Do you like it?'

'You look like the tabby moggy next door to us. But yeh, I guess it's cool.'

'It cost a fortune.'

'You mean you had to pay to have that done to you?'

'It was a bit of a mistake really.' I tried to justify the price by mentioning the ten per cent off.

'So what are you going to do with the money you saved, send it to Oxfam?' asked Chuck.

'Tell me, does your brace hurt?' I said, by way of changing the subject.

'Murder, but a guy like me can take that kind of pain.'

'Mine's agony.'

'You're not going to be much good in childbirth,' observed Chuck.

'I am never, just never going to have children. I've a very low pain threshold. Some people have, you know.'

Chuck looked concerned. 'You could always have an epidural.'

Chuck's mother is a medical secretary, so he's really knowledgeable about all this technical stuff.

'What's that?'

'It's an injection of anaesthetic into the central nervous

50

system. It numbs you from the waist down. You don't feel a thing.'

'An injection!' I wailed. 'If there's one thing I can't stand it's injections. Seriously, I'd rather die.'

Then we got talking about phobias and things and how I used to have this absolute terror of the dark and had to sleep with the landing light on because of ghosts. And Chuck started to go on about ESP.

'I'm not talking about weirdos who see flying saucers and things,' he said. 'It's just a fact that there's a whole spectrum of existence that is totally unexplored territory. I mean if you think of time and space as one vast galactic program. . . .'

Chuck was latching into 'scientific mode' and I was rapidly losing interest. It was on the tip of my tongue to interrupt and tell him about Juste. Chuck's really a positive genius about maths and physics and stuff. I mean, literally, for the first twelve years of his life no-one saw anything but the back of his head as he clung like a limpet to his computer terminal. At one point he even devised a way to hack into the Mansard Hall computer system. I used to go into the Computer Studies Room and switch on to find deeply embarrassing messages appearing on the screen like:

'Hey baby . . . you just turned me on!'

Or even more cringe-worthy:

'Justine, my dream/delectable icecream/top of my menu/ my disks go all floppy over you.'

There were further messages I'd rather not go into.

Mr Clyde, our part-time computer teacher—a deeply impressionable male with an unfortunate tendency to blush— seemed to find the erratic behaviour of his AppleMac terminals incredibly disturbing. Then someone complained to Noddy that they thought our system had a virus—and she made a random spot-check just when one of the most unfortunate messages was up on the screen—after that Mr

Clyde left, quite suddenly, mid-term.

Anyway, to come back to Chuck, I decided then and there not to confide in him, despite the fact that he could probably come up with an incredibly logical explanation for Juste's appearances — it just wasn't worth the risk.

So I said instead: 'Do you fancy sharing a free-range Mars Bar?'

Chuck shook his head disapprovingly: 'All that refined sugar, Justine, pure exploitation.'

So he settled for a bowl of Coco Pops instead — heavily post-rationalised by saying he didn't think anyone had yet come up with a way of intensively farming rice . . . he was a bit vague about the cocoa beans. He was deep into his second bowl when the phone rang. It was Franz.

'What do you mean. Don't come round now? Who have you got there?'

'Just a friend.' I couldn't explain to Franz or anyone that I just knew it would be so excruciatingly embarrassing if Chuck and any member of the Pack met. I mean, it hadn't been a problem when we were younger; we generally met somewhere neutral, like Queen's Saturday Skating or the Hammersmith Odeon or something. But just lately he had, for some unaccountable reason, taken to dropping by at my place. I just prayed his visits wouldn't coincide with theirs. I just couldn't face the culture clash.

Franz started to make a big deal out of this *friend* I had found. I could tell Chuck was listening in although he was trying to look as if he wasn't.

Before I could stop him he took the phone from me.

'Well, hello there,' he said, putting on this deep mid-Atlantic accent.

'Who are you?'

Chuck gave a brief, if exaggerated, run-down of his height, colouring, GCSE potential and general sex appeal.

'Maybe we could meet some time?' he finished, confirming my worst fears.

'Maybe,' said Franz, with barely suppressed enthusiasm.

I reclaimed the phone. 'I'll call you later, OK?'

Of course, after that it went right round the Pack that I *was friendly with* this mega-hunk. I couldn't help noticing that my rating went up quite a bit, so I kind of played along with it. My failure to introduce Chuck to them was interpreted as quite natural possessiveness. The problems didn't occur till later.

In the meantime, from my point of view, the fact that Chuck kept on ringing me up and dropping in only served to reinforce the difference between this sort of relationship and *the real thing*.

I know I didn't see an awful lot of Sebastian, but the few glimpses I did catch (my heart usually did a kind of suicide-leap and made an uncomfortably heavy landing) confirmed in my own mind that He was the one and only one I would ever—positively ever—feel anything for. The only problem was—how to let Him know how I felt in a suitably charismatic way.

Absolutely nothing occurred to me *until* February 14th loomed threateningly in the Filofax—the dreaded St Valentine's Day, that annual festival invented by card manufacturers specifically to mortify people like me. In fact it was Juste who suggested that a suitable card directed towards Sebastian might be the ideal way to make him subtly aware of my presence.

She was filing her finger-nails at the time, they were now the kind of length I had wild dreams of achieving and painted a dazzling Day-Glo green. She was using what looked like a miniature buzz-saw.

'What on earth is that?'

'Haven't you seen a nail file before?'

'Not one like that.'

'No, I suppose you haven't. It's running down actually. When are you going to stop biting your nails, by the way?'

'I have,' I said, rapidly moving my hands out of sight.

'You could have fooled me.' She moved the chewing gum to the other side of her mouth and lit a cigarette from the one she was smoking, then said:

'Look, this Sebastian guy—you could sit at home and die of old age before he noticed you.'

'Yes, but don't you think a Valentine is a bit naff,' I said.

'How else are you going to let him know? Thought transference?' she asked.

'But how will he know it's from me?'

'You'll have to give him some clue, nothing too obvious. Just some little thing that gives a strong enough hint without totally giving the game away.'

After she'd faded out I sat for a while wondering why Juste was being so insistent. It wasn't until later that it occurred to me, with a deep sinking feeling in the stomach, that maybe there was something in her past love life (and more importantly—my future one) that needed changing. I grabbed my purse and headed off up the King's Road.

W H Smith had its usual pre-Valentine's Day crowd of sheepishly amorous people hovering around the birthday card display and making furtive forays into the Valentine section. I double-checked that no-one from school was in sight and then made for the largest and most expensive cards. I selected one with a great big padded red satin heart in the middle. It cost an absolute bomb . . . But, after all, wasn't my entire future at stake?

Back home once more, I sat with pen poised waiting for inspiration. The message inside the card simply said, in curly gold script: 'Be mine'.

I was tempted to leave it at that and just post it. But Juste was right, there was absolutely no point at all in wasting all that money on a card if Sebastian would have no idea who it had come from. On the other hand, a blatantly obvious Valentine would be too seriously tasteless.

At last, I merely added the letter 'J'. At least that would single me out from people with names that started with the other twenty-five letters of the alphabet. Just to add a further hint, I posted the card in the Cheyne Walk post-box.

The next day I received my usual very thinly disguised humorous card from Daddy. He might at least try and alter his handwriting!

And one which could have only been from Chuck. It had a picture of a warthog with a bow in its hair and said 'Wallowing in pash' inside.

School was a pain that day as everyone compared notes. Leonie had surrounded herself with a huddled circle of admiration. She claimed to have received ten cards which she displayed when challenged.

I admitted, truthfully, to having two, and was heavily cross-examined as to who they could be from.

'But you must have some idea,' said Henry.

Max added: 'Maybe one of them's from HIM.'

'No way,' said Franz. 'That kind of guy wouldn't stoop to sending a Valentine to anyone.'

'What do you mean?' demanded Leonie.

'Boys who send Valentines are generally short, spotty and socially insecure,' said Franz.

Leonie looked decidedly miffed at this and went off to display her cards to the Dregs who provided a suitably awe-struck audience.

Apart from the card count, St Valentine's Day provided another challenge—the Heartache Ball, scheduled for the following weekend. Simply everyone was going to it.

Naturally, my mother had been doing everything possible to ruin my social credibility. She had a real paranoia about Non-Charity Balls. Initially, she had said a categorical 'No'.

But I had been working on the indoctrination for months. Finally, worn down by my carefully applied parental torture, she had announced:

'Well, you're not going to one of those terrible Balls without a partner.' And she added, 'They're not properly chaperoned. Anything could happen.'

I recognised this as the first step in her climbing down.

'But Mummy, everyone is going. There'll be a whole gang of us.'

'And anyway you're too young. I said fifteen was the absolute lower limit. This is the thin end of the wedge.'

The 'thin end of the wedge' was one of her favourite expressions. It was an umbrella phrase which applied to virtually anything—anything worth doing.

At fourteen and three-quarters I realized that the only way I was going to be allowed to go was to give in on some point.

'All right I'll go with a boy. But who?'

My mother made some quite ridiculous suggestions. The son of one of her bridge friends, for instance: Hugh of the pink ears and wet hands.

'I would rather not go, frankly, if it has to be Hugh.'

'Then how about Chuck?' she suggested.

'He wouldn't want to go. And anyway, he couldn't afford a ticket.'

'I'm willing to pay for him,' said my mother.

'I'll think about it,' I said, playing for time.

My mother, luckily, didn't recognise this parody of one of her own favourite prevarications. 'I'll think about it,' was a phrase she fell back on quite often. It was alternated with the stronger: 'I'll have to ask your father.' If his answer was negative she had another exasperating expression: 'Your turn will come.' This, I hated most of all. It was generally used to refer to something Jemima was allowed to do and I wasn't. I had long been resigned to the fact that my turn never did come. Or by the time it did, I had more than likely ceased to want to do whatever it was.

The following morning she caught me at a weak moment when I was struggling to emerge from the depths of slumber with a glass of mango and guava juice.

'It's all arranged,' she announced triumphantly. (Her voice is always incredibly loud in the morning.)

'What is?'

'Don't mumble, darling . . . About the Ball, Maggie says Chuck would love to go with you.'

It's staggering how insensitive parents can be.

I complained to Juste about it. She was surprisingly un-sympathetic.

'So what's wrong with Chuck anyway?'

'Everything! The things he wears, the things he says, he's too thin and he's got a brace.'

'So have you.'

'No need to rub it in.'

'But he's male, isn't he?'

'Marginally.'

'You're just going to have to brave it out, Baby. Maybe he's got hidden depths.'

Why was she being so nice about Chuck? I suddenly had this fleeting horror vision of him, most probably bearded by then, lurking limply somewhere in the background of Juste's apartment.

'Juste. I've got to ask you something . . .' I started.

'Umm?'

It was on the tip of my tongue to ask the unthinkable—what if Juste told me that I had ended up with Chuck and that we were even *married* or something! I mean, I'd have to live the rest of my youth in deepest gloom with this hideous fate looming over me.

'Nothing,' I said. I had this growing conviction that once I was told about the future I was going to think those things were simply bound to happen. Like reading about diseases in Mummy's *Miller and Keane's Medical Dictionary*—and thinking I'd got them.

So I added hurriedly:

'Whatever is going on in your life, remember, I simply don't want to know!'

She shrugged. 'Charming!' she said.

7

The night of the Heartache Ball happened to coincide with the last day before half-term. Approximately two-thirds of the Fourth Form were going to it, *ie* all but the Dregs.

Henry had booked the fifth floor loos and was giving French manicures at 50p a time. Franz had doused her hair in Sun-In and was hanging backwards out of the Fourth Form window trying to catch some stray ray of weak February sun. A couple of girls were heating wax over Bunsen burners in the Chemistry Lab and waxing their legs in the darkroom.

The teachers wandered around distractedly sorting through piles of lost property and trying to kindle some enthusiasm for half-yearly exam results. My new pair of Reeboks turned up unmarked, unworn and outgrown.

I had been given the job of cleaning the Art Room sink. A girl called Sam, who wasn't actually part of our Group but who was really almost bearable for a Non-Descript, had offered to help me so that she could get some peace to pluck her eyebrows.

'So what are you going to wear?' asked Sam.

'My mother made me buy this frilly green shot-satin off-the-shoulder ball dress from Fred's. Real protective clothing. It comes down practically to my knees.'

'You're not seriously going to wear that?' said Sam.

'I'm going to go in it, just to keep the Poor Dear happy. But I'm taking this really cool strapless mini-sheath of my sister's and changing in the loo.'

'What's it look like on?' said Sam, gazing at me critically.

'It's OK as long as I remember to keep my stomach in.'

'Won't your sister mind?'

'Jemima need never know. She's been sent to France for half-term on a last ditch French revision crash course.'

'When's she getting back, anyway?'

'Not sure, end of the week I think. Why?'

'Apparently some male was asking about her.'

'Oh really. Who?' I found Jemima's many conquests rather tiresome.

'Sebastian Something double-barrelled.'

My stomach did a double-somersault.

'Sebastian Symington-Smythe? How do you know him?'

'I don't. My brother met him at a Ball in the country.'

'He lives in our street.'

'That's right. Apparently he told my brother that your sister has got this big thing about him.'

'What an ego-tripper. She doesn't even know him.'

'She must have seen him around.'

'Maybe.'

But why, I asked myself, should Sebastian think she was interested in him? As far as I knew she'd never even spoken to him. Then, quite out of the blue, I had a lightning vision of my Valentine. 'J', it had said inside.

Oh my God.

I scrubbed at the Art Room sink with more vigour.

With unconscious sadism, Sam increased the agony.

'So, we're all going to meet this hunk of yours tonight?'

'Who?'

'This Chuck guy you've been keeping from us.'

60

Since Franz had spoken to him on the phone, Chuck had become a kind of Fourth Form legend. I had been trying for some days, unsuccessfully, to trade down on the Form's current expectations of him. In hunk-rating, the gulf that stretched between Sebastian and Chuck was immeasurable. You might as well be comparing Rob Lowe to Woody Allen. No, that's not entirely fair, Woody Allen has a certain charm.

'I'm not sure if he's going to turn up,' I said, wondering wildly if I could find some way of putting him off with tact and diplomacy.

I rang him as soon as I arrived home from school.

'Listen Chuck, honestly, are you sure you want to come tonight? I won't be hurt if you want to back out.'

'I was starting to look forward to it, actually, in a masochistic kind of way.'

'It's going to be full of awfully posey people, ball dresses and everything.' Then a thought struck me: 'You know it's black tie, don't you?'

'Justine?'

'Yes.'

'Will you calm down? I've got it all under control.'

'Are you sure you haven't been forced into this?'

'I told you, I want to come.'

'Promise me one thing.'

'What?'

'You won't dance with me, will you?'

'Justine!'

I rang off.

Franz, Henry and Max were all changing at my place.

Franz arrived first with her stuff crammed into her school

61

bag. My mother eyed the bag uneasily.

'But where's your dress, Francesca?'

Franz pulled out something which closely resembled a crumpled bin liner.

'Would you like me to run an iron over it for you, dear?'

'Thank you, Mrs Duval. But it kind of stretches when it's on, so the creases fall out.'

When the others arrived we were all force-fed with spaghetti. Would you believe it, she had actually put garlic in the sauce! I think she does these things on purpose.

This left us with a mere two hours to get ready.

Why is it, just when you want everything to be perfect, fate turns against you: the razor attacks your legs, tights snag, nail varnish smudges, the mascara brush dries out and your blusher totally goes to pieces in the washbasin?

Ten minutes to zero hour, we were passing round the Gold Spot when Max, who was leaning out of the window trying to dry the glue under her stick-on-nails, said:

'There's some guy at the door.'

It was so typical of Chuck to be early.

Franz, whose dress was so tight she gleamed like a wet seal, hobbled to the window and leaned out.

'I can't see,' she complained.

Henry wriggled between them.

I shot downstairs to remove the object of their scrutiny from the doorstep. I wanted to check him over before they came down.

My father had already collared him and was pouring out a low alcohol lager.

They were deep into some argument about privatisation. I had never been able to understand why my father liked Chuck, all they ever did was disagree.

'Gosh Justine, you look almost like a girl,' said my father. 'What do you think, Chuck?'

'Pretty fantastic. I would hardly have recognised you.' Chuck went a bit pink at this point. Then, suddenly realizing the unfortunate nature of the comment, he made it worse by adding: 'I mean, it's not that you don't always look OK, but I'm not used to seeing you all done up like that.'

I thought it best to ignore this ill-chosen phrase.

'Daddy, aren't you going to give me a drink?'

My father disappeared downstairs to mix a judiciously watered-down punch.

Chuck was wearing a DJ several sizes too large but almost presentable. From there on down, everything deteriorated: his usual black 501s had had creases carefully ironed into them but beneath these I caught sight of his dreaded pink and silver Nike trainers.

'You can't, you simply can't go like that,' I hissed.

'Wrong colour socks?' asked Chuck, feigning innocence.

'Those disgusting *things* on your feet!'

'My mother's fault. She forgot to pick the others up from the menders.'

'But couldn't you have borrowed some, or something?'

'How many people do you know with size twelve feet?' asked Chuck.

I made him keep his feet under the coffee table when the others eventually descended and we all made polite and forced conversation with my parents over the punch.

Surprisingly enough, Chuck seemed to get on quite well with the others. Franz had spotted his Greenpeace badge and had started a totally uncharacteristic conversation about whales—or was it seals? Some underprivileged aquatic mammal, anyway.

My mother didn't notice Chuck's offending footwear, she was too distracted by the appearance of my girlfriends.

'Of course, everything was so different in my day,' she said, casting meaningful glances at the exposed length of

Franz's legs. 'At your age we were actually dying to be allowed to wear long evening dresses and put our hair up. These days it's all the other way round.'

'You mean skirts up and hair down . . . Gosh that sounds like a toast. Cheers everyone,' said my father, in a valiant attempt to infuse some party atmosphere.

I don't think Mummy thought this was funny in the least.

8

My mother insisted on driving us to Le Palais in the Volvo. We made her stop and let us out in Hammersmith Broadway but it was pretty humiliating all the same. Outside there was a large gathering of people greeting each other with a lot of kissing on both cheeks. (For quite a time my mother thought this is what 'French-kissing' meant; it seemed such a pity to have to disillusion the poor innocent.)

We spotted about a dozen people from our class, the ones with boys who were anything worth looking at were hovering on the pavement in the light to be sure that no-one missed the treat of seeing them.

I hurried my small party through the doors as quickly as possible, hoping not to be observed in my green atrocity. I noticed that Chuck was causing a slight wave of interest. I didn't discover why until later.

Inside, the Mafia was there in force. A couple of their pin-thin girls were giving out information about the next Ball. The Boss hovered by the main entrance between two of his henchmen, surveying the scene with his ice-blue eyes and selecting the occasional deeply-favoured person to shake by the paw.

Clasping the bag with Jemima's dress in it, I headed

straight for the loo. That's when I bumped into Him.

'Hi there, how are you?'

He looked so absolutely edibly scrumptious in evening dress I would have happily died for Him then and there if I could have thought of a suitably stylish way to do it.

'Fine,' I managed to breathe.

'Is your sister with you?'

I explained how far away Jemima was and wished her even further. Then I dived into the loo to divest myself of the despised dress.

'Why, oh why,' I questioned the mirror, 'did He have to meet me then?'

'Who was that?' said Chuck when I rejoined him.

'Sebastian Symington-Smythe,' I said. 'He lives in our street.'

'A friend of yours?'

'No, yes, sort of. Why?'

'Looks a bit of a wally to me.'

Such overt male counter-tactics weren't worth acknowledging, so I merely replied: 'What do you think of the dress?'

'What was wrong with the other one?'

I gave him a withering look: 'You simply wouldn't understand.'

A few minutes later Max came up to me and whispered hoarsely in my ear: 'He's here! Sebastian Thingummy!'

'I know,' I said. 'I've spoken to Him.'

And I started to dance with Chuck in order to avoid further questioning. It wasn't until we were in full view of everyone and I trod on his toe that I discovered why Chuck was causing so much interest.

'What's happened to your trainers?' I shouted over the music.

'I left them in the car.'

66

'You did what!'

'I didn't think you liked them.'

'You are impossible.'

The evening wore on. The air grew thicker with cigarette smoke. The atmosphere hotter, the music louder. Assessing the average age of the revellers, the barmen had started demanding ID for anything alcoholic.

Chuck riffled through his pockets and produced his bus pass.

'That proves that you're under eighteen, not over it, you idiot,' I pointed out.

Couples were starting to pair off and drop out in crumpled heaps against the walls. Most of them were boarding school kids who had just been let out for the holidays. It appeared they had several weeks of smoking, drinking and snogging to catch up on. The over-enthusiastic were already being chucked out by the bouncers and were hanging around the doorway looking sheepishly pleased with themselves, and trying to get back in again.

Chuck would insist on dancing near me. He has this really nightmarish way of dancing. It involves just about every part of his body and takes up a lot of room. I was trying to dance quietly by myself and pretend he wasn't there. But he kept writhing up to me and smiling encouragingly which made the laser lights glint on his brace and really drew attention to us.

We had run out of money for drinks quite early on, even Cokes cost a fortune, so we were reduced to getting glasses of tap water from the loo. On one of these trips, threading my way through the assortment of limbs strewn across my path, I bumped into Leonie. She was leaning against a pillar smoking a cigarette with one hand and holding a half-full champagne bottle in the other, looking bored.

'Oh hi, Justine. Having a good time?' she asked without interest.

'Brilliant!'

'We were just about to move on, really. Going somewhere with a bit more life. See you around.'

Sebastian approached out of the gloom. His tie was undone and His shirt was open showing a small but delectable area of gleaming all-season tanned chest.

'Come on then. If you want a lift to the Wag, let's go,' He said to Leonie.

He draped a possessive male arm around her backside.

She stalked off, positively purring with satisfaction.

As they disappeared through the doors He turned, swung his jacket over his shoulder and winked at me. My knees went to jelly, He was so deliciously arrogant.

Max, who had been observing their departure from behind a column, came over and put a sympathetic arm through mine.

'Obviously a sex maniac,' she said dismissively.

Actually, it would have been kinder to have pretended not to notice.

I fetched my glass of water and decided to find some haven where I could avoid both the Pack's sympathy and the risk of a dance with Chuck. I selected the balcony which looked over the dance floor. There were quite a few couples up there far too engrossed to take any notice of me.

Cigarette smoke curled up through the coloured laser shafts. Down below the mass of dancing bodies pulsated to the throb of the music. The mirror ball scattered its confetti of light specks into the void. But somehow the glitter had gone out of the evening. I caught a fleeting glimpse of Franz. She had had this bet with the others about who could get off with the most boys. The prize was a bottle of Malibu which we'd all chipped in to buy. Basically, I was out of the running because of my brace. I don't like Malibu anyway, I can't stand coconut.

I wondered without much hope whether Franz had got off with Chuck. I doubted it, Chuck went to a co-ed school and had got the whole snogging thing out of his system years ago. He was into 'meaningful relationships'—not that he could find anyone to have one with.

I stared dismally at the mammoth screens which were projecting a video of a little-known and unlikely-to-get-better-known-group. The screen fizzed with static and then cut in on one of the singers.

In that instant I recognised Juste.

She was wearing incredibly short hot pants and miming— slightly out of sync—the words of the song.

Suddenly, she caught sight of me and stared fixedly in my direction. 'Hi Mouse!' she mouthed.

I felt myself flush scarlet as I imagined everyone in the building must instantly turn their attention on me.

No-one did.

She winked and smiled. I noticed something was different about her.

Her teeth, the brace. It worked! I couldn't help feeling a glow of satisfaction. It might not seem world-shattering to you—but I had proved beyond reasonable doubt, that I had some control over my destiny.

Juste was gesturing earnestly at me to get down on the dance floor and dance. She was obviously petrified I was losing credibility points sitting on my own like this.

I shook my head.

She took a few steps nearer the camera. I felt as if at any moment every eye would turn on me. I gave in and headed down the stairs that led to the dancers.

Downstairs the outskirts of the ballroom had begun to look like the outer limits of hell on an average day. However, a fair number of dancers were still swaying dutifully on the dance floor.

I brushed past a blond boy with a crew cut.

I had to impress Juste by dancing with something good-looking. The blond boy was definitely too young.

I made another small circuit of the tables and spotted a boy who appeared to be on his own, who looked almost presentable.

'Excuse me, could you tell me the time?' I asked. (OK I know—that was so corny!)

'No idea, sorry,' he said and turned his back on me and started talking to the boy beside him.

Over on the far wall I could see Juste was still observing me with a frown.

'How would you like to buy me a drink then,' I heard myself say.

'What a cheek. Shall I buy this young woman a drink?' he asked his friend.

'Why not?' he said.

I tried to ask for a Coke. But thanks to a glance from Juste, it came out as, 'Bacardi and Coke—and make it a double!'

After this things got a bit out of hand. The 'almost pre-sentable' boy suggested dancing, so I gulped the drink down and headed for the floor. Actually, he was a pretty cool dancer and I hoped Juste was watching because I felt I was dancing in a pretty cool mode too. That is, until the ballroom started to do unaccountable whizzing things every time I turned. I think that's maybe why I tripped. The dance floor was pretty crowded by then and as we hit the floor we must have caused a bit of a pile-up.

I think that might have been when the photographer took the picture.

Anyway, the next thing I knew was that Chuck was ex-tricating me from the tangled arms and legs of all those people who had landed on top of us.

Chuck said he thought it was time we left.

My mother was outside waiting for us in the Volvo looking like thunder. Apparently, we were half an hour later than the one o'clock deadline we had promised to keep to. Franz and Henry and Max were already in the car making polite conversation.

I sat squeezed in the back with them feeling miserable and a bit sick as we drove home and Chuck went on about the destruction of the ozone layer.

My mother still hasn't got round to having the Volvo converted.

9

I suppose my parents might never have found out about it if it hadn't been for the conservatory. They only take *The Times, The Telegraph* and, very occasionally, *The Independent.*

The man who was constructing the conservatory (Mrs Duval's Crystal Palace as he calls it) takes a certain tabloid that Daddy refers to as *The Rag*. He was reading it with his sandwiches when my mother took him out a kitchen mug of Nescafé.

A minute or so later she was standing in my bedroom rousing me from my essential eight hours in the most inconsiderate manner.

'Justine!'

I raised myself on one elbow.

'What are you doing with *The Rag* . . .' I started . . .

'WILD CHILD ANTICS OF HOORAY HENRIETTAS' read the headline. Beside it was a rather jumbled picture of bodies, the identity of one of them was unmistakable. I wasn't looking my best.

'Oh my God . . .' I started. 'Listen, I can explain everything.'

I remember what followed as a somewhat stormy morning. The phone rang a lot. Franz, Max and Henry got up

quietly and hurriedly and went home without having breakfast. My mother went back to bed with a cup of weak Earl
Grey and two Valium.

Chuck rang at around eleven.

'Have you seen the papers?' I asked.

'I know, live bugs in London tap water. It's disgusting,
isn't it.'

'No, it's me. I'm in *The Rag*.'

'The what?'

I explained.

'Where, Page Three? I'll have to dash out and buy one.'

'Chuck listen, this is serious. I'll probably get expelled or
something.'

'They haven't exposed the dire nature of what you girls
make in the Chemistry Lab, have they?'

'Shut up and listen . . .'

Chuck thought the whole thing was terribly funny.

'Mummy says it's probably totally ruined my future.'

'Guess you'll have to become a social dropout like me.'

Actually, Chuck had voiced my deepest innermost fears.

We were interrupted by a wild and familiar ringing on the
doorbell. I hung up and went to answer it.

It was back.

Through the spyhole Jemima, weighed down by bags of
French booty, was looking travel-stained, dishevelled and as
stunning as usual.

She leaned on the bell again.

'Hi Bratface. Can you do something about the cab? I've
only got French francs.'

I took a fiver out of the cab fare box on the side-table. (The
cab fare box was one of Mummy's ways of protecting our
virtue—'It's never too late or too far to get home, girls.')

'I'd forgotten you were due back today,' I said.

'Thanks. Where is everybody?'

'Daddy's at work, Mummy's in bed and I'm in dreadful trouble.'

'Preggers?'

'No, worse.'

'You failed all your mid-year exams?'

'Much worse.'

I handed her *The Rag*.

Jemima practically hit the roof. I'd forgotten that I'd been wearing her dress.

'And you can jolly well pay to have it dry cleaned,' she said over the conciliatory breakfast I cooked for her.

'What are we going to do about Mummy?' I said.

'You'll have to do penance and be incredibly sweet and helpful,' said Jemima. 'Wear a skirt or something. She's had blows like this before. Don't you remember when I refused to be a Deb?'

'You'd better go and see her,' I said and I made another cup of weak Earl Grey.

Penance took the form of tidying out the toy cupboard. Mummy had been threatening to send everything to Oxfam—even the furry animals!

By mid-day I was well into deep and moving rediscovery of my youth. As year upon year of toys had accumulated, the cupboard had formed a kind of strata from which I could trace back into my formative past.

By around two o'clock I had penetrated down to the wooden Galt educational toys: unbroken, unused and un-loved.

I suddenly became aware of being observed.

My mother was standing in the doorway in her Laura Ashley housecoat.

'I had to opt out of the blind dogs' coffee morning,' she said reproachfully. 'I just couldn't face it. That frightful picture!'

'At least the blind dogs wouldn't have seen it,' I said.

'Justine. This is no joking matter.'

'Sorry Mummy.'

I offered her a large bag of toys for her Conservative Bring-and-Buy.

'These are all clean, presentable and with no bits missing,' I said.

'All right, the rest can go to Oxfam,' she said, peering into the bag. 'I don't know what your father's going to say.'

'But nobody we know reads *The Rag*,' I said.

It's staggering how wrong one can be. A little before two-thirty the phone started ringing. By that time my fellow revellers had risen and those who had actually achieved a relationship serious enough to exchange telephone numbers were engaged in the ritual post-Ball promenade of their conquests along the King's Road. Very soon the World's-End-to-Belgravia jungle telegraph had spread last night's gossip up as far as Sloane Square.

By the third telephone call it became clear that I had achieved a kind of global fame—and with so little effort on my part. However, with wisdom beyond my years, I was already starting to recognise the essential distinction between being famous and infamous. It was clear something had to be done to retrieve my wilting reputation.

I arranged to meet the Pack at Daquise. Daquise is a small Polish tea room in South Ken where absolutely no-one ever goes. It would provide the ideal venue to plan our counter-attack.

By the time I arrived, Henry, Max and Franz were already there drinking lemon tea.

'I think you can take off your dark glasses now,' said Franz. 'They all look like *Guardian* readers to me.'

'How can you tell?'

'Hand-knits and horn-rims.'

When my eyes had adjusted to the gloom of the café, I caught sight of the bottle of Malibu protruding from Franz's bag.

'What was the final score?' I asked.

'Twelve and a half,' said Franz.

'Twelve and *a half*, how come?'

'One of them was contested, Henry claims I kissed the same boy twice. Anyway,' she added dismissively, 'no-one else scored over four.'

At that point Max brought out the offending copy of *The Rag*. She spread it out on the table:

'It really does look like an orgy, doesn't it? It's tough luck you feature so prominently.'

Several heads turned in our direction.

Franz bought me a slice of chocolate gateau, but I hadn't the heart to eat it.

'You mustn't let it get you down,' said Max, sympathetically eating the gateau for me. 'We'll all stand by you.'

'What were you proposing to do? Ring up the entire readership of *The Rag* and give them a rundown on my sweetness and innocence?'

'Perhaps we could get you an appearance on "Wogan", so that you can clear your name,' suggested Franz.

'Fat chance,' I said. 'Maybe the most effective thing would be to march up and down the King's Road in a sandwich board.'

'Or we could spray paint messages on walls: "Justine Duval is innocent",' suggested Henry. 'Like they did for that chap in the East End.'

The lady at the next table was starting to exhibit a more than natural curiosity in our conversation.

'But seriously,' I said, lowering my voice. 'It's absolutely beastly for Mummy. She'll be torn to shreds at the next Parent/Teacher Committee Meeting.'

'Why don't we simply ring up the paper and put them straight,' suggested Franz. 'Maybe they'd print an apology or something.'

'Brilliant. It should give the name of the journalist who wrote the article,' said Henry, who started leafing through the pages.

'Kathleen Kemp,' she announced.

Henry got *The Rag*'s number from Directory Enquiries and then we all huddled together in the café's tiny phone booth.

I put on my best 'Assembly Announcements' voice.

'Could I speak to Miss Kemp please.'

'Who shall I say is calling?'

'Justine Duval.'

There was a pause.

Then a mid-Atlantic growl announced: 'Kathy Kemp, who's that?'

'Justine Duval.'

'Justine who?'

'Justine Duval, you had a picture of me in your paper this morning. The one at the Ball.'

The voice made an abrupt change up to mid-Atlantic charm.

'Why hello, what can I do for you?'

'It's just that you've got it all wrong. I mean, you've given a really false impression.'

'Really?' she was trying to sound convincingly surprised. 'Maybe we should get together for a chat? Where are you now?'

No sooner had I mentioned Daquise than she said:

'I know it. Don't move. I'll be right with you.'

I put the phone down.

'I don't believe it. She's just going to drop everything and come over here.'

'She must be feeling really guilty,' said Max.

While we waited, I started to wonder whether this had been such a good idea. There was something about her keenness that made me feel uneasy.

'Well, how else are you going to clear your name?' asked Franz.

At last a taxi drew up and a middle-aged woman in a three-quarter-length black leather coat climbed out. She was followed by a chap in jeans carrying a camera.

She made straight for our table.

'Hi! Call me Kathy,' she held out a hand. 'Now which of you is Justine?'

We were told not to mind Mike (the photographer), who had really just come along for the ride and wouldn't take any pictures unless we wanted him to.

Kathy ordered more lemon teas and gateaux all round.

'I can see we're going to be friends,' she said.

She started just by asking us general things like whereabouts we lived and what school we went to.

I was careful not to give my actual address, but Franz let out that we went to Mansard Hall.

Then we got on to what we did in our spare time and it all sounded terribly tame.

'But surely good-looking girls like you have boyfriends?' she prompted.

'Not really. We have boys who are friends, but not actually boyfriends.'

Then we just went through general things likes parties and sleep-overs. And how strict our parents were. In fact, I was a bit embarrassed about how tame it all sounded. And I think Max was too, because she got a bit carried away and exaggerated how much champagne she'd drunk at her brother's

Eighteenth. So I moved the conversation on to a safer subject and we chatted about clothes and pocket money and the kind of music we liked—she noted quite a lot down about that.

I didn't quite see what it had to do with clearing my name, but Kathy seemed to find all this boring stuff fascinating. Then Mike took a few pictures, 'just for the record', and they shook hands with us and left.

I went to sleep that night praying that while we'd put the record straight we wouldn't come out sounding like a load of wimps. So it was with some trepidation that I crept out before breakfast and bought a copy of *The Rag*. The front page headline read:

LURID LIVES OF SEX-STARVED CHAMPAGNE CHARLOTTES

And beneath it was a picture, a very clear picture, of Max, Henry, Franz and myself.

I hurriedly folded the paper in two and slipped a *Telegraph* over the incriminating pile beneath it. I couldn't look the newsagent in the eye as I handed over the money.

At home, I locked myself in the bathroom and sat down on the floor praying that the article didn't live up to the headline.

There followed a graphic description of all-night parties and lurid movies (this must have been Max's artless mention of us veg-ing out in front of a *Teenage Mutant Hero Turtles* video!). I felt my face go scarlet and the hairs on the back of my neck stand on end as it went on to mention how we were heavily into Acid (we meant Acid House music but somehow it didn't come out sounding quite like that). Franz's description of what she had been wearing had been transformed into 'emerging from her Eaton Square address in skin-tight black leather'. And her particular style of dancing was described as 'exotic'. There was more: Henry denting her brother's car at their country cottage became 'reckless under-age driving in their country acreage . . .'; Max's three glasses of champagne became 'drunken debauchery while the heedless parents looked on . . .'

I read the article once more. If you read each bit really carefully you could see that it had been cleverly contrived so that most of the things said were quotes from us which could be interpreted in more than one way.

This did not alter the fact that we were all now in dire trouble. I knew I was being cowardly, but I really couldn't face calling the others. I decided to sit tight and wait until the storm broke.

In the meantime I racked my brain for some way round the problem. Basically, I only came up with two solutions. The first was to get a bank loan and buy up every copy of *The Rag*. The second was to hijack a space shuttle and leave the planet.

I don't really want to go back over that day. The first three hours were spent experiencing the deepest darkest anguish known to man—that of being guilty of an undiscovered crime. I've never read *Crime and Punishment*, but I saw a couple of episodes of the series on television and now I knew just how that poor guy felt.

I even absent-mindedly unloaded the dishwasher for my mother without being asked, so you can see how deeply I was suffering.

At around eleven, the phone rang. My mother answered it.

'Yes . . . Oh hello . . . (surprised tone). How are you?'

(Pause)

'No, I haven't (self-righteously). We only take *The Telegraph* and *The Times*.'

(Long pause)

'I see . . .' (spoken really slowly).

(Longer pause . . . I could detect a frantic tone in the voice at the other end.)

'I'll ring you later, Selina.

'JUSTINE . . . !'

While the storm actually raged I felt somehow relieved, as if some of the responsibility had been taken out of my hands.

When she had finished with me, my mother spent a long time on the phone to my father. There was a lot of talk about solicitors and suing . . .

'What do you mean, Davison will charge a fortune?'

'. . . . .'

'Travers . . . I know they've been very foolish. But you do realize, this could blight Justine's future. She'll never be asked to be a Deb now!'

'. . . . .'

'But what about me? And Jemima?'

'. . . . .'

'People have been known to win libel cases!'

'. . . . .'

'Well, I'm relieved to hear it!'

Then my mother slammed down the receiver and retired to bed with a migraine.

I rang Henry.

She was extremely cool on the phone. Apparently Franz's mother had rung her mother as well. She made some transparent excuse about a dental appointment and rang off.

I rang Max and was told she wasn't in.

Then I rang Franz.

'The thing is,' said Franz, 'they all feel this would never have happened if it hadn't been for you.'

Clearly, there was a certain amount of truth in this.

'How are your parents taking it?' she asked.

'It might have been marginally worse to have been exposed as a mass-murderer.'

'Same here,' she said.

'How about going to a film or something tonight?'

'No chance, I've been gated. And my allowance has been suspended.'

'Hea-vy.'

'Look, I've got to go now. Don't ring me, I'll ring you,' said Franz. Then abruptly, she rang off.

I threw myself down on the sofa. I didn't even feel like turning the television on, I simply couldn't face Juste at present. When she got to hear about this she'd be down on me like a ton of bricklayers.

Then Jemima came in and turned it on anyway.

'Honestly, you're just sitting there. You could at least record "Neighbours" for me! You know I'm trying to work,' she said. And she strode out of the room to make some intense long-distance French-male-orientated phone call upstairs.

Before I could switch off, Juste caught me. She had edited herself in sitting at Madge's dining table; at least she'd edited her head in, her body was wearing the most grotesque pink acrylic tracksuit with appliqué gum-nuts embroidered on it.

'Would it help to talk about it?' she asked in a 'Neighbourish' tone.

'So you know what's happened?'

'It just slipped into my memory.'

'What do you mean?'

Juste looked at me as if I were being incredibly dense.

'What you do now is in my past . . . Right?'

'Right!'

'So obviously, I can remember it!'

'I see . . .' I said, trying to get my mind round this one. 'So you know what a mess I'm in?'

'Naturally.'

Then came the surprising bit. For once Juste was actually

quite sympathetic.

'Look,' she said, 'basically there's no such thing as bad publicity. If you don't want to end up a nobody, you'll have to learn to weather it out.'

'But it looks like I've become a social outcast. I mean, the phone hasn't rung for at least an hour! No-one wants to speak to me!'

'So . . . find a new set of friends.'

'It's not that easy.'

The pink acrylic tracksuit rose from the table and, complete with Juste's head, started to do domesticated 'Neighbourish' things in the kitchen.

'Wanna-bet?' said Juste.

At that point Jemima swept back into the room, still breathless from her call.

'Who the hell is that?' said Jemima. 'Honestly, it was bad enough when they changed Beverly—I can't keep up!'

Luckily, Juste caught sight of Jemima and faded herself out so that Madge's head resumed its rightful place.

'What do you mean, who's that?' I demanded. 'It's Madge.'

Jemima stared at the screen like a bemused cat.

'You feeling OK?' I asked. 'How's Jean-Pierre?'

'Di-vine,' sighed Jemima and instantly forgot everything else.

I was right about being a social outcast, however.

It took a couple of days for all the Mansard Hall parents to cotton on to the fact that Justine Duval—wild child of West London—was not a good influence on their darling offspring. For the time being at least it seemed my name had been erased from London's social diaries. So much for the eternal bonds of friendship.

The atmosphere at home was pretty frosty too.

Daddy was furious because the solicitors said there weren't enough grounds to sue, but were sending him a large bill for their advice.

Mummy was furious because she said she would never be able to look anyone who knew us in the face again. Not to mention all the people who didn't. Jemima still hadn't got over the fact that half the world had seen her black sheath dress before she had even worn it.

The last straw came when the news eventually percolated through to Noddy. My parents were summoned to the school for a quiet but intense discussion. The outcome of this was that I was suspended—indefinitely.

I was sentenced to exile in the country while everything cooled down. This took the form of an undefined period at 'Trudgings', Little Walping—Grandma's Norfolk home.

The very last thing that happened before I left was that the phone rang.

'Can I speak to Jemima?'

I would have recognised His voice anywhere, but I answered automatically with the standard telephone answering technique that had been so painfully brainwashed into me by my dear sister.

'I'm not sure if she's in, who's calling please?'

'Sebastian Symington-Smythe,' He said. Oh that poetic alliteration!

'Sebastian Symington-Smythe,' I repeated, just for the pleasure of saying it, 'hold on, I'll see.'

I could hear Jemima's Jane Fonda work-out tape on full blast upstairs. I had to think fast. I did some running on the spot noises and opened and closed the sitting room door a couple of times.

'No, sorry, she seems to have gone out,' I said.

'If I give you my number, can you ask her to give me a call

84

or leave a message on my answerphone?' He said.

I dutifully took a note of the number in the secret section of my Filofax.

'Don't forget now,' He said.

'I won't,' I said.

Then I left to catch my train.

IO

The train hauled itself out of Liverpool Street station and headed through the desolate tracts of outer London. I gazed out at the lines of blackened buildings with their blind nicotine-clouded windows. This was the flip side of the city. Each rear view was riddled with drainpipes, cross-hatched by fire escapes, displaying tangled cables and rusting central heating outlets. London had turned its back on me.

Soon the city terraces were replaced by identical rows of semis, huddling side by side with their lean-to DIY garages and their limp lines of washing turning grey in the drizzle. As the train gathered speed I caught glimpses of ragged allotments—the first threatening signs of encroaching nature.

My heart sank: from now on all was to be green, mud-clogged and damp. Luckily, I had armed myself at the station with this month's *Vogue*. I drew it out of my bag and opened it, breathing in that profoundly comforting aroma of freshly-printed page.

By the time the last vestiges of civilisation had given way to soaked fields, with their damp cows dutifully chewing flavourless cud, I had worked my way through every reassuring glossy page of ads and read all about 'Island-hopping in the Seychelles' and noted all the forthcoming 'Hot Spice

Colours' for 'Heady Summer Days'. I'd discovered that, with the incredibly freaky insight of horoscopes, the fact that I was having trouble on the 'home front' and was now involved in 'essential travel' had long been 'on the cards', and there were some pretty nasty predictions about my financial situation as well. Then I came to the 'Men in Vogue' section.

The train took wing—it slid like some gilded creature across an idyllic landscape with lush fields shaded by downy clouds—playing soft rhythmic music as it went.

Sebastian S-S smiled up from the page. It was a casual half-smile, showing just enough of His perfect white teeth. The suit He was wearing hugged His body in soft folds of cashmere, His scarf hung in breathless suspense on the wind. I turned the page. He scowled divinely at me, taking no interest whatsoever in the female model who was attempting to entwine her body around Him. The fashion feature went on with Sebastian looking infinitely desirable in a cricket sweater and blue jeans, mean and moody on a Harley-Davidson in a biker jacket . . .

I was so lost in the magazine that I hardly noticed we were drawing into Norwich station. Suddenly, I saw the familiar figure of my grandmother waving from the barrier. I hastily gathered my belongings and landed on the platform.

'Hello darling.'

I kissed the soft folds of her cheek. 'Hello Grampy.'

She stood back and looked at me.

'Well, yes, you do look a bit peaky.'

My mother's excuse for my urgent exodus to the country had been my failing health. This suited Grampy, she loved nothing better than a bit of morbid illness. Fresh-air-and-exercise was her cure for everything from chickenpox to piles. I thought grimly of the countless country weekends from which we had returned with sore throats and hacking coughs to be nursed back to health on Benilyn and central heating.

'Had a good journey, Poppet?' Then she added, without waiting for a reply, 'I hope you've brought plenty of thick woollies.'

We climbed into her Morris Minor with its familiar smell of dogs and bone meal and lurched off.

'Do you mind if I open a window, Grampy?' By association, the dog and bone meal smell had brought an instant return of childhood car sickness.

'That's right. Get plenty of fresh air,' said Grampy, grinding into second gear.

We drove out of the town into the gathering gloom. The car was soon engulfed by narrow close-hedged lanes. Moisture dripped from straggling hawthorn, sodden cow parsley slapped against the car's wings. The dog and bone meal smell was gradually drowned out by the rich stench of fresh manure.

After a nauseous half hour, 'Trudgings' approached through the dusk. I climbed out and swung open the big white gate. The car lurched through, dousing me in muddy water from a conveniently placed pothole.

'Welcome back,' I said to myself and followed the car's stately progress as it squelched down the drive.

In the icy porch, the mingled scents of geranium leaves, Mansion Polish, Harpic and, fainter but still distinguishable—drains, brough memories flooding back.

All those endless, sunless summers with Jemima playing Monotony or Squabble (as we had renamed them). All those walks in ill-fitting gumboots when Grandad tried unsuccessfully to interest us in the various names of trees and birds and other tediously rural things. And how all this contrasted with the glimpses of bright blue skies and glinting seas which would arrive in the form of postcards from our parents who had gone off to places that were far too hot, or too far, or at any rate *totally unsuitable* for us.

Then I came back to earth as I heard Grampy say, from force of habit, 'Down Gambol, good dog.'

Gambol limped geriatrically towards me and took a half-hearted sniff: the days had long gone when he could summon the energy to jump up at anyone.

'There, I've put on both bars and it will soon be nice and warm,' said Grampy, ushering me into the living room.

Gambol and I made for the hearth-rug and jockeyed for position nearest the two glowing electric elements.

Nothing had changed. There were the same Baker chintz loose-covers in which I used to find faces in the flowers and the same fraying bobble-fringed lamp shades. The standard lamp still leaned at its drunken angle, and the photos of Grand-dad and Grampy still stood close by one of Mummy in her Queen Charlotte's Ball outfit, and the one of Mummy and Daddy looking *almost* young and ferociously optimistic at their wedding. Then there were ones of Jemima and myself in various formative stages of our youth. English seaside ones, where we stood obediently under-clothed, smiling and goose-pimpled, and one of Jemima on horseback at the time when she had fallen briefly but passionately in love with ponies before she discovered boys.

After a supper of lumpy asparagus soup and ancient meat-loaf, I helped Grampy wash up. I'm sure she could afford a dishwasher, it was sheer perversity on her part to continue with this outdated ritual.

'It's no wonder you're looking peaky,' she said. 'You don't eat enough. Look at your mother, look at me . . . We're not intended to be thin in our family.'

I looked at Grampy's large form clothed in its copious Gor-ray skirt and Jaeger jumper, and felt really depressed.

Then Grampy said we might as well 'tuck in' as the television had been playing up earlier that evening.

'Playing up? How?' I asked.

'Peculiar interference. Some odd woman kept appearing, probably foreign. I blame it all on the Common Market and those satellite saucer things they're sticking up everywhere. I'll ring the repair shop tomorrow and complain, it quite ruined "Gardener's World".'

So at the unholy hour of 10 p.m. we both went to bed.

Grampy had left a pile of *Horse and Hounds* and *Country Lifes* next to my bed. I scanned through, trying to make myself dozy, wondering how this alien species of human being in their Puffas and headscarves survived the miseries of country existence. By one-thirty I was driven under the covers by the cold and put out the light.

I had forgotten the total pitch blackness of the country night. Outside my window an owl hooted, it was a mournful noise. I huddled further down the bed. I fell asleep only to be reawoken some minutes later by an eerie wheezing and knocking. Trudgings' antiquated plumbing announced to the world that Grampy had just pulled the chain.

Velvet darkness surrounded my bed, peace reigned.

'Lovely morning. You don't want to waste all your holiday in bed, do you?' The curtains screamed along the rusty runners as Grampy let in the ashen dawn light.

'What time is it?'

'Almost eight. I let you sleep in.'

Grampy had run me a bath of the most amazingly hot water straight from the Aga. So hot that by the time I came downstairs I was the colour of cheap Canadian farmed smoked salmon.

'There you are, you see,' said Grampy. 'A little country air and you look better already. After breakfast you can have a nice long walk.'

I gazed out of the kitchen window.

'But Grampy, it's raining.'

'Nonsense,' said Grampy. 'Just a slight drizzle. It'll soon pass over.'

It didn't. It continued throughout that week. Not without variations of course: slight drizzle, heavy drizzle, rain, heavy rain, heavier rain and total uninterrupted downpour.

Despite the weather I had several 'nice long walks', from sheer desperation. I snooped around the village shop a couple of times. Honestly, there wasn't anything with a brand-name I even *recognised*, apart from a lone Mason Pearson hairbrush in a battered cellophane box. But this was understandable if you studied the target market. I was starting to form a theory: that everyone young, beautiful, or in any way stylish had abandoned the country long ago and headed for the cities. What was left was a kind of sub-species of humanoid identifiable by its pastel acrylic knitwear and Hush Puppies and insatiable appetite for seed catalogues.

Five of the longest and most featureless days and un-memorable nights passed before, just as I returned from one of these damp sorties, the phone rang.

'Justine?'

It was only Chuck.

'Oh hello . . . what are you calling me here for?'

'I'm in the school call box . . .'

'We'd better be quick then . . .'

'No worries. I've done the phone-tapping trick. How's everything? Enjoying the local *Wild Life*?'

'Ha . . . ha . . . No need to rub it in. Is this just a social call or what?'

'Actually . . . I was after a phone number . . . your friend Franz's.'

'Oh yes . . . why?'

I caught myself feeling just the teensiest twinge of posses-siveness. I mean Chuck might be a wally—but he was my wally.

'She said she was interested in helping me with my Save the Whales petition.'

Now I knew for a fact that the nearest Franz had come to an interest in marine life was how to bone a sole elegantly at a restaurant table.

'Really!'

'You sound surprised.'

'Oh no . . . not at all . . . It's 071 . . . 358 . . .' He dropped the phone twice before he managed to write it down.

Then he simply said: 'Thanks a lot.' And rang off.

I put the receiver down. I had this sudden vision of life moving on in London and leaving me out of the action. It was as if I'd died or something and while suffering the excruciating tedium of heaven, I'd had a glimpse of what was happening in the real world below, without me—I mean, Franz and Chuck!

I think this must have really got to me because Grampy caught me skulking in the kitchen raiding the chocolate biscuit tin. She said I looked worse and suggested a dose of liquid paraffin . . . as if I were an out-of-fuel fondue set or something.

That evening the phone rang again.

'Hi Bumpkin. How's life in the House of Horrors?'

It was Jemima.

'Oh, much as usual. Strange and inexplicable noises throughout the night. We're virtually cut off by knee-deep puddles. Crippled animals limping round all over the place.'

'Poor Gambol.'

'It's Grampy's fault, she simply stuffs him with sponge cake.'

'You getting nicely fattened up?'

'I expect so. Grampy's scales gave up the ghost years ago. How's the situation back home anyway?'

'What situation?'

'The Press situation, you idiot.'

'Oh boring, boring. I think everyone's forgotten all about it,' said Jemima dismissively.

'So why are you ringing. This can't be mere sisterly love?'

'I just wanted some information, that's all.'

'About what?'

'About that guy who goes around with Leonie.'

'Who?'

'Sebastian Thingummy, you know, the one Mummy can't stand.'

I tightened my grip on the receiver.

'Why?'

'Oh, no reason in particular.'

'No information then.'

'OK. He's asked me out, that's all.'

'When?' I asked. This came out as a sort of choking noise.

'Friday night, after the exams finish. You all right?'

'Where to?' I continued, fighting to control my voice.

'Only for a drink. Why the inquisition?'

'Mummy'll kill you.'

'Mummy won't know, we're meeting in Sloane Square.'

'I see,' I said, my mind racing.

'Well, what do you know about him?' she demanded.

'Well, for a start, he was chucked out of school.'

'What for?'

'Probably drugs or perhaps because he's gay, there's still a lot of prejudice in public schools you know,' I said.

There was a pause while this sank in.

' . . . At least that's what Franz told me; her brother went to school with him so he should know,' I added for effect.

'But I heard he took Leonie out,' Jemima said.

'He only gave her a lift to the Wag where he left her with a massive bill for drinks. He's a real woman hater apparently. He just abandoned her. She had to borrow some money to get a taxi home.'

I didn't add the rest of the story which had filtered my way—apparently Leonie had insisted on being bought champagne and then had flirted outrageously with every male in sight in a futile attempt to make Sebastian interested.

'So they're not really going out?' Jemima sounded ominously pleased at this piece of information.

'Well, they are and they aren't.'

'What's that meant to mean?'

'Oh, she's just one of the mass of girls he's tagging along,' I said. 'After all, he is a male model.'

'Is he?'

'He's all over "Men in Vogue", positively puke-making.'

'Oh . . .' said Jemima, sounding even more exasperatingly impressed by this. Then she added as an afterthought, 'By the way, Noddy called and apparently you're going to be allowed back to the land of the living.'

'Really!' It was typical of Jemima to leave the essential information till last.

'Mummy'll be ringing to confirm, so you'd better start looking healthy or something.'

When she'd rung off, I wandered into the kitchen and put the kettle on to make a cup of tea. But my mind was on more important matters. It wasn't until I'd screwed the top on to my hot water bottle before realizing I'd pre-heated it and added two measures of Darjeeling that I noticed how absent-minded I was becoming.

Back in the sitting room with the nicely brewing bottle for comfort, I curled up with *Vogue* open at my favourite picture of Sebastian, my mind racing.

Through force of habit, I must have switched on the television.

With a fizz of static, Juste came through.

She was wearing a Barbour and had her hair scraped back under a Hermès scarf of the horseshoe-and-stirrup variety topped by a pair of sunglasses. The effect was slightly marred by a strand of violently tinted hair which had escaped from the scarf.

'What on earth are you wearing?' I asked.

'Thanks to you, I seem to be stranded here in the country. I'm having to try to look conventional,' she said.

'How come?' I asked.

'Don't you see how everything you do in your life affects mine? It seems you went to a polo match and for some un-fathomable reason fell for this . . . this . . . *jerk in jodhpurs!* . . . You formed some sort of eternal bond . . . and I've been stuck with him ever since!'

'But I haven't been anywhere near a polo match!'

'Well, for God's sake do something. I can't stand it any longer. I'm even starting to talk about horses and dogs—I'm virtually moulding away from rising damp!' she said, light-ing a cigarette.

'I wish you wouldn't smoke so much, you must be ruining my lungs,' I complained.

'There's simply nothing else to do down here,' she said. 'You've got to get back to London and put some concen-trated effort into finding a decent boyfriend . . .'

'Like who . . .' I started.

She shot a meaningful glance at *Vogue* and said: 'How's it going with him, for instance?'

'Oh. He's not really my type.'

'What's wrong with him?'

I snapped the magazine shut. I wasn't going to bare my sacred innermost thoughts to anyone—not even myself.

'Anyway,' I continued, 'it looks as if Jemima's interested in him.'

95

'Defeatist,' said Juste.

'No I'm not.'

'If you're keen on him, go for it. You only live once,' she said.

I frowned. I felt Juste was being insensitive about my deeply cherished private feelings.

'Well, don't blame me if you end up with some sort of retard in riding boots,' said Juste.

'But what shall I do about Jemima?'

'Sabotage!' suggested Juste.

'How?'

'You're in a prime position, well behind enemy lines. Use your ingenuity!'

I was about to ask for more detailed guidance when Grampy ambled into the room.

'There it is again!' said Grampy as Juste dissolved in an electronic fizz. 'I'm ringing Grundles Repairs first thing in the morning.'

I went to bed early, busily plotting the next stage of the campaign to capture Sebastian.

By almost midnight I still hadn't come up with an even half-decent idea and I fell asleep.

With morning came enlightenment. I arrived at the breakfast table to hear Grampy shouting into the phone in the tone of voice one only ever uses to an answering machine:

'It's fizzing . . . foreign interference . . . probably danger-ous . . . Trudgings . . . Little Walping . . . and would you please come and collect it this morning.'

'Who's that, Grampy?'

'I was trying to explain to one of those dreadful machines what was wrong with the television,' she said.

It was then that it occurred to me how unidentifiable

people sound on answerphones.

As luck would have it, I had to stay in and wait for the television man while Grampy went off to do some unspeakable task involving dung and ditches.

The first couple of times I rang Sebastian's number he answered with a heart-stoppingly sleepy voice, so I rang off.

I waited for an hour or so and my next call found him out. With breathtaking casualness his recorded voice said:

'This is Sebastian Symington-Smythe . . . I'm sorry I'm not here to take your call, but if you would like to leave your name and number after the tone I will call you back . . .'

I went all wobbly inside after that and simply couldn't say anything, so I had to call the number again.

At last I managed to speak fairly clearly—I think in a pretty good imitation of Jemima's voice—after the tone:

'Hi Sebastian . . . This is Me! . . . Awful drag but I've got to be somewhere tediously central on Friday . . . Could you meet me in The Ritz Bar instead . . . Same time . . . OK? Must dash . . . See you then . . . Bye.'

If I had estimated correctly The Ritz Bar would have absolutely staggeringly expensive drinks, and it would also be an excruciatingly embarrassing place to be stood up in. I also calculated that waiting in Sloane Square with all the world seeing no-one turning up would be equally humiliating for Jemima.

Grampy threw open the front door, bringing in a blast of air fresh with ditches and dung, to find me looking very pleased with myself.

'There, you're looking much better already. Which is good because guess what? . . .' she said.

'What Grampy?'

'There's polo on Saturday and a whole load of the young from round here are going.'

(POLO!)

'Well, I don't actually feel that much better,' I said hastily.

It was at that point my mother rang.

So then I had to feel better again—much better.

I managed to arrange the actual timing of my release for Friday afternoon, which would give me time to '*prepare-for-school-on-Monday*'. It would also mean I would be able to observe the success of my 'Jemima/Sebastian' plot at first hand.

As soon as everything was fixed I rang Franz with the good news.

'Oh that's brilliant . . .' she said with about as much enthusiasm as a soggy Weetabix.

'So what's everyone doing this weekend?' I asked.

Franz hesitated just long enough for me to get the message—or was I getting paranoid? 'Oh . . . things . . . not a lot. Anyway . . . see you at school on Monday.'

I tried hard not to let Grampy see how delighted I was to be returning to London. I think I made quite a good job of it too.

'Such a pity you have to go back so soon,' she said as we stood on Norwich station. 'Apart from the polo, we've got the Annual Festival of Bell Ringers on Sunday and you'll miss all the fun.'

'It's been terribly good of you to put up with me. It's done me so much good,' I croaked, hoping she wouldn't notice my sore throat.

Grampy observed my pink, chapped face with affectionate pride.

'Nothing like fresh country air to put you back on your feet,' she said.

As the train pulled out of Norwich station I settled into the corner seat and closed my eyes.

'Back to civilisation!' I said to myself.

II

I splurged on a cab back from Liverpool Street. With any luck I should be passing through Sloane Square at around the time Jemima was expecting to meet Sebastian.

Sure enough, as we rounded the corner into the Square, I caught sight of Jemima standing in a very short skirt beside the Monument, trying to look nonchalant.

I leaned forward and tapped on the cabbie's window.

I held out my twenty pound note (Grampy's parting gift — 'buy yourself a nice outfit from me, Poppet' — honestly, inflation seems to have totally passed Grampy by).

'Do you think you could just cruise up and down the King's Road and round the Square again till this is used up?' I asked. I wanted to be doubly sure that my plot had worked.

The cab managed to take in two circuits of Sloane Square and each one revealed Jemima looking more dark and thunderous than the last. It was just starting to rain when we made the third round trip, so I asked the driver to slow down and shouted through the window:

'Want a lift?'

Jemima gave me a glower of recognition and stalked over to climb in beside me.

'What on earth are you doing standing in the rain?' I

questioned innocently.

'Don't ask!' she steamed. 'Don't speak to me!'

'That's a nice welcome home!'

We drove on in silence and when I'd paid off the cab and we were both inside, Jemima said:

'If anyone rings, particularly anyone male . . . with a name that happens to start with S, I'm not in. Right?'

'Right,' I said.

He rang about twenty minutes later.

There was a faint suggestion of a piano playing in the background and that slightly breathless sound, as if suffocating in thick carpets, that hotels always have.

'Is Jemima there?'

'No she's not,' I said obediently as instructed. 'Can I take a message?'

'Yes you can . . . It's Sebastian. You can tell her I waited for a good hour and twenty minues and I've gone home. Right?'

'Right,' I said.

Jemima's face appeared over the bannisters.

'Was that him?'

'Yes it was. He said he waited for a good hour and twenty minutes and has gone home.'

'Who does he think he's kidding?' said Jemima, and slammed her door.

It worked!

The next day was Saturday and from sheer force of habit I headed for the King's Road to check out the Saturday night scene. Outside Gossips I caught sight of a group of familiar figures. Max was lighting up a cigarette and Franz was sitting with a boy kind of draped artistically around her shoulders. Henry had her back to me. I waved frantically and Max looked up and then turned and said something to Franz. I had a distinct feeling that they didn't see me on purpose.

I toyed with the idea of leaping off the bus and saying 'Hi there!' but something instinctive inside told me that this was a particularly rotten idea. As the 22 made its hesitant way forward a great nostalgic wave of Saturday memories flooded through me—like trudging in a crowd through damp streets to track down a party which we weren't let into because there were too many of us. Like eating baked beans off burnt toast in someone's kitchen with the extractor fan on full so their parents wouldn't sniff out the Marlboros. Like the soothing dawn chorus of Walkmans as we all tried to get to sleep after a really freaky horror movie and, in the background, the sound of Max throwing up in the bathroom. It was hard to take being cut off from all this. In fact, deep down, it hurt a lot.

Thoughts like these were still running through my head as some way further down the King's Road we passed the Mafia car, parked on a double yellow line. I could see the Boss busily talking into his car phone. A load of female Mafia groupies were loosely arranged around him trying to look suitably laid back.

Then, a little further still, I caught sight of Chuck. He was hovering on the kerb in a pretty typical wally-ish pose, unable to make the epic decision about whether to cross or not.

'Chuck!' I screamed at him through the window—which just shows how starved I was for human contact! As luck would have it the bus had just stopped at some lights, so I leaped off.

'Justine, I thought you were still in exile.'

'I've been allowed back: time off for good behaviour.'

'Where are you going?'

'Nowhere in particular.'

'Then you can help me choose a present for Franz.'

'For Franz?' Then I remembered. 'Of course, it's her birthday soon, in fact . . . today.'

'Umm, should be a pretty cool evening . . . I mean . . . (Chuck caught sight of my face) You have been invited?'

I shook my head.

'You haven't?'

'I don't think Franz's parents like me very much any more.'

'What creeps. I shan't go then,' said Chuck.

'Don't be mental, of course you must.'

'Well, I think that's really rotten.'

'Oh, it doesn't matter, I've got better things to do tonight, anyway,' I said, tossing up between watching television and hiring a video.

'I still think it's rotten. Maybe they think you're still in the country.'

'Most probably,' I said.

We went into Tiger Tiger and Chuck chose a stuffed walrus for Franz. He actually wanted to buy her a dugong but the saleswoman said there wasn't much call for dugongs—and what was a dugong anyway?

Chuck went on for quite a long time about their habits, habitat and distinguishing features. The sales assistant suitably enlightened, we left.

I paused outside for a moment with Chuck shifting his weight indecisively from one trainer to the other, wondering what to do next. So I put him out of his misery by saying I had a hundred and one things to do and couldn't hang around. As I merged into the King's Road Saturday crowd he stood on the pavement waving the walrus's flipper after me.

I walked on several hundred yards trying to ignore what a nerd he looked, wondering what on earth to do with myself. I hadn't the heart to go to Gossips. I couldn't face braving the stares in Oriel. I didn't even fancy a pancake in the Dutch Pancake House. So I simply headed on towards World's End and it struck me for the first time what an incredibly depressing name 'World's End' was. So I turned and walked back the other way.

I decided that as things stood the world had more or less come to an end anyway. Justine Duval might as well cross herself off the social calendar and become a total recluse. I tried to think of the most reclusive thing I could possibly do. Chelsea Library loomed ahead of me. I slipped in between the polished mahogany doors. As they swung closed it occurred to me that I still hadn't started the research I was meant to be doing on my GCSE Religious Knowledge project. I made my way towards the shelves marked Divinity. I defy anyone to get much more reclusive than that.

When I had selected a pile of the thickest and most acutely dull books I could find, I had a little altercation with the librarian over my library ticket. Had I ever had one? Probably not. She wouldn't accept my On-Line card and made me fill out reams of forms and provide double ID.

As I pointed out to the poor dear, it was quite honestly worse than getting a Harvey Nichols account—and for a few measly pre-owned books too. I don't think she took too kindly to this.

Anyway, if it hadn't been for my RK project I don't think I would ever have joined the Mafia. It was just one of those flukes of fate that I happened to be walking down the Library steps trying to balance this enormous pile of books when the Mafia car drove up. I mean one can't ignore the Mafia car. It's this enormous bright pink 1950s American Cadillac with massive tail-fins. I was just about to cut through down a side street that led back to Cheyne Walk when I became aware, out of the corner of my eye, that the car was driving along very slowly by my side.

An electric window slid down and a voice shouted:

'Hi, you look like you could do with a lift.'

I nearly dropped the books from shock.

Then I realized it was Jason—Franz's half-brother—who was driving.

'What on earth are you doing driving that thing?' I asked.

'The guy who owns it's lost his licence so I've started chauffeuring for him—pretty cool car, eh?'

I tried not to look too impressed.

'A bit ostentatious if you ask me,' I said.

'It goes like a bomb, he's had something done to the engine.'

'Really?'

'Climb in and see.'

So I did.

'I suppose you're going to my kid-sister's party tonight?' said Jason between bouts of making roaring noises with the accelerator.

'Well, I haven't really decided yet. I might have better things to do.' I wasn't going to admit I hadn't even been invited.

Jason cast an assessing eye over me. He slowed the car down. 'Do you mind if we stop off for a moment? I've got to check something out with some people?'

He swerved across in front of the on-coming traffic, ignoring the furious honking and shouts from cabbies, and screeched to a halt outside Ed's.

'Hang on here, I won't be a moment.'

I was left in the car while Jason dived inside.

I watched him with half an eye through the window as he talked to a group of typical Mafia hangers-on. I could tell that he was talking about me because a couple of them turned and stared with more interest than I've ever seen the Mafia exhibit. My starring role in *The Rag* had evidently not gone unnoticed. I was starting to feel uncomfortably like a modern-day Christine Keeler. This was what it must be like to be Big, Bad and Not Nice to Know. I groped in my bag for my shades and settled further back in the seat hugging my pile of books.

That was when I saw the Pack approaching from the Sloane Square direction. I felt my face flush scarlet behind the sunglasses. I saw Franz lean over and whisper something to Henry and I could tell she was making puking noises like we always did when we saw anyone doing anything particularly posey. I pretended not to notice and waved in a superior way and they all sort of half-waved back and crossed the road so that they passed on the other side.

At that point Jason climbed back into the car.

He pointedly ignored the fact that his half-sister was making a spectacle of herself on the other side of the street and said:

'Well, if you're not going to Franz's nursery tea party, why don't you come with us and help hand out invitations tonight?'

Out of the corner of my eye I could see Henry bent double with helpless giggles at something Franz had said.

Jason glanced down at my pile of books. The title of the top one read: *Persecution and Martyrdom in a Christian World*.

'That's if you haven't anything better to do,' he added.

'OK, why not,' I said.

That evening, Jemima made history by actually answering the phone herself. I had practically fallen downstairs in an effort to get there first. So I was sitting on the bottom step rubbing my twisted ankle and couldn't help overhearing the conversation.

'You couldn't have done, I waited for nearly an hour . . .'

'. . . . .'

'You don't expect me to believe that?'

'. . . . .'

'That's a blatant lie.'

'What are you doing hovering in the hall, darling?'

My mother swept down the stairs in a cloud of Estée and Daddy's last year's Christmas present—the mink.

'Nothing.'

'Well, I don't think it's very nice to eavesdrop on Jemima's telephone conversations.'

'*You* do.'

'Nonsense, anyway that's totally different, I'm her mother.'

At that point Jemima slammed down the receiver and swept past us.

'Who was on the phone?' my mother mouthed at me.

'No idea,' I said.

'Caroline, you can't go like that. You'll get lynched.' My father was standing at the top of the stairs looking down.

'Am I a bit OTT?'

'The fur! . . . Isn't this "do" we're minders at in aid of World of Wildlife?'

'Heavens, I thought that was next week.' My mother fled upstairs to change.

'I wish Mummy wouldn't wear fur,' I said.

'Mink is factory farmed,' said my father.

'Isn't that meant to make it worse, not better,' I pointed out.

'Anyway,' my mother was calling from the bedroom, 'I hope you two won't be getting up to anything tonight. We don't want any more trouble, do we?'

'Franz is having a sleep-over,' I called back. It was the truth after all. I just didn't mention the fact I hadn't been invited.

'Well, do try to get some sleep,' said my mother, offering a freshly Charles of the Ritz powdered cheek.

'Have a brilliant time,' I said.

And they sailed out leaving the coast clear.

It was hours before I was due to go out so I wandered into our sitting room, turned on the television and spread myself out on the sofa.

A woman in a skin-tight scarlet evening dress stared back at me. It was Juste.

'It's Saturday night for goodness' sake, Justine. You're not going to simply stay in and watch television, I hope?'

'No, as a matter of fact I'm being taken out in a massive pink limousine with enormous tail-fins.'

'That's more like it,' she said. She peered out of the set. 'Shouldn't you be getting ready or something?'

'I am ready,' I said.

'You're not going dressed like that?'

I was wearing my latest pair of Joseph Tricot leggings, a new grey hooded top and a sweatshirt artfully knotted round my waist. I even had on the super-cool pair of Cons I had managed to filch off Henry for thirty five quid.

'This is Power Dressing, man,' I replied. 'And it happens to be my newest and dearest . . . anyway, what's wrong with it?'

'Well, if you must go around looking like a badly wrapped parcel . . .' she said.

'Everyone I know dresses like this!' I broke in.

'Precisely!' she said. 'And who was the one who didn't want to be like everyone else?'

I had to admit she had a point there.

'So what would you suggest?'

'Something black, short and tight,' she said decisively.

'Juste . . .' I objected.

'Well, don't ask my advice then. And see how you'll end up.'

107

'All right, I'll go and see if I can find something else to wear,' I said grudgingly.

'That's more like it. Have a good time!' And with that Juste faded herself out.

A quick look through my wardrobe revealed the truly dire nature of my situation dress-wise. Jemima shot her head round the door and said:

'Right I'm off. Have a good time and mind you don't get sick on jelly and ice cream.'

I had half a mind to tell her where I was actually going and then thought better of it. She headed down the hall and left, slamming the front door with her usual abandon. It wasn't until she was half way down the street that I discovered she'd gone out in my only black mini-skirt.

Revenge is sweet. The mysteries of Jemima's wardrobe beckoned. I started to go through the umpteen little black dresses wondering which one would fit me. I'm a bit larger than Jemima which she is never at a loss to point out. However, my legs are a good two and a half centimetres longer which I seldom fail to mention in reply.

The third little black dress was the stretchiest, and as long as I kept pulling it down it was perfectly respectable. I tried on a pair of Jemima's high heels too, which weren't too bad when I was standing up straight and posing but made me look like some sort of hump-backed wading bird when I tried to walk in them. So I rejected these in favour of my Cons.

That's when I heard the lovely sexy throaty noise of the Mafia car outside. There was no time for eye make-up so I threw on Jemima's Wayfarers and charged downstairs.

There were three other girls in the car. I hadn't been prepared for this. They took in every detail of what I was wearing in one lightning assessing glance and then talked among themselves.

When I look back on that evening it came out as a sort of nightmare. During the brief interludes when I wasn't being totally ignored I ended up having agonising conversations talking to people at cross-purposes. Most of the chat was about who they knew and where they'd been for the past days-nights-weeks, and since I didn't know anyone they were talking about and hadn't been anywhere, I soon found it wisest to simply keep quiet and listen. I hoped they might interpret this as being super cool. But I think they simply forgot I was there. I was relieved when we all ended up in the most incredibly noisy club called Crazy Something and no-one could hear anything anyone said anyway.

Jason bought us all drinks and he must have seen my face when he brought out this great wadge of notes with a rubber band round it to pay for them.

'It's not all mine,' he said. 'It's ticket money.'

'Ticket money?'

'Yeh, for Energy nights. You ought to see if you can sell some. For every ten you sell you get two free and if you can sell those too, you can make quite a bit.'

'Really?' I said. I was getting interested. I still owed my mother for the Ball ticket money I had splurged on the hair-cut. And then there had been a few other essentials. I kept on stalling her by saying no-one would pay up and she was getting to the stage when she was threatening to call their mothers. It was all rather fraught.

So I said, 'That sounds like a brilliant idea.'

Anyway, after that we all bundled into the car and drove to the Grosvenor House Hotel. They were having one of those Balls that Mummy absolutely relishes which are 'properly chaperoned'. I'd suffered quite a few of these in my 'formative youth', dancing with boys about half my size who've only just got into their first pair of long trousers and have voices that are still at the stage of making up their minds

about gender. Jason and I stood outside as the youthful revellers started to trail out and search blindly for their Mummy's or Daddy's cars. We'd lost the other girls ages ago in
some club or other, so Jason and I were in sole charge of
handing out the Energy flyers and were doing so fast and
furiously, thrusting them into damp little party-going hands
and trying to make sure that none of those innocent little darlings slipped the net.

I was just handing one to a boy who looked particularly
well-washed behind the ears when I heard a little scuffle
behind me.

'Who has given you permission precisely?'

I recognised the voice of Mrs Ponsonby-Haugh.

'Oh my God,' I said and reached for the Wayfarers.

I grasped the cigarette Jason was smoking and under the
mistaken impression that I could hide my identity behind a
kind of smoke screen, I took a deep puff and blew out a cloud
of smoke. It was awfully funny-tasting smoke.

'Justine!'

It wasn't Mrs Ponsonby-Haugh's voice this time, it was
worse.

It was *my mother's*.

Nobody had told me that the World of Wildlife 'do' she
and Daddy had volunteered to be 'proper chaperones' for
that night was at the Grosvenor House.

I was swept into the Volvo and suffered the entire ride
back under a torrent of parental paranoia.

12

The outcome of this little episode was a total clamp-down on funds and I was gated for two whole weekends. Also I had to vow absolutely never to see 'those people' ever again.

I rang Chuck about it. I didn't want to go headlong into my tale of woes, so I started by saying:

'Hi there, it's me, Justine. What are you doing with yourself?'

'At this precise moment in time? . . . to coin a cliché.'

'Well yes . . .'

'I'm cutting little crocodiles off my leisure-wear.'

'De-Lacoste-ing them, why?'

'I want to wear them for soccer practice, don't fancy getting mobbed.'

'Could you save the crocodiles for me?'

'Sure thing . . . what on earth for?'

'To sew on my games gear . . . Mummy bought me anonymous Peter Jones's *again*.'

'Zero cred-rated . . . won't do for Mansard-Whores . . . eh?'

I ignored North Thames Comprehensive's vulgar abbreviation of Mansard-Hall-Girls. (We call them The Gas Board for more reasons than I'd like to go into.)

'Quite . . . anyway, what are you doing with Lacoste? I thought it was against your religion?'

'Present from Franz—but I guess that's history now.'

'Say, how was the party?'

'Oh it was cool. At least to start with . . . that is, until Franz and I got locked in the bathroom.'

'Locked in the bathroom! How come?'

'Well, we were all playing this game of Strip Trivial Pursuit. I mean, I would have been OK if there had been questions on Quantum Mechanics or something, but I kept getting naff sorts of things like "How many dimples are there on a golf ball?" or "Who won the FA cup in 1969?" I think Franz was rigging it.'

'That still doesn't explain about the bathroom . . .'

'I was getting to that. Well, Franz and I had got down to virtually the minimum, I mean one garment each . . .'

'!'

'It's OK, she was in one of those all-in-one body-suit things . . . when we heard the key in the lock!'

'Her parents!'

'Heading back early from the last act of *Siegfried* . . . the philistines . . . Anyway, Franz just dragged me into the bathroom and locked the door.'

'I don't think I want to hear what happened next.'

'After a lot of rattling and shouting through the door her stepfather opened it with a screwdriver. You see it had one of those little screw things on the outside that you can open in an emergency like a kid locking itself in or something . . .'

'OK, OK, I get the picture! What did you do!?'

'Well, we both had kind of wrapped ourselves in bath towels which I suppose, in retrospect, if anything made it look worse. And her stepfather bawled at Franz—"Who is this individual?"'

'What did she say?'

'She said I was a friend of yours.'

'Thanks a lot, Franz.'

'And I really thought I was getting somewhere with her,' added Chuck with a sigh.

I restrained myself from commenting that a lot of guys felt that way.

'She's even given the walrus back,' he said gloomily. Then added: 'Maybe a guy who wasn't an "utter cad" would return the leisure-wear.'

'I don't think she'd want it back without the crocodiles.'

There was a thoughtful pause . . . then Chuck said:

'Anyway, what did you get up to last night?'

I had a sudden insight—if Chuck and the Pack had a culture clash . . . Chuck and the Mafia had a double-double-culture clash!

So I said: 'Oh, not a lot really.'

If only this had been true. When Chuck had rung off I sat for a while reflecting on the truly dire nature of my current life—or lack of it.

What really rubbed it in was the way Jemima was putting herself about. One thing I've never understood about parents is their incredible double standards. Things that are practically unmentionable at fourteen for some reason become perfectly acceptable at eighteen. Jemima had already reached this golden age.

Once her A Level exams were over she lapsed from doing virtually nothing to doing absolutely nothing. She lived an enviable nocturnal existence which meant our paths seldom crossed. Occasionally, roused at dawn by the contented purr of a cab receiving payment, I would meet her on the stairs, fresh from some Ball or night club—bright-eyed, flushed and smoked as a kipper.

By day, she lay like a large maggot, cocooned in her duvet

with the portable phone as a life-line to the outside world. She would emerge only when absolutely necessary to record 'Neighbours' or to browse through the fridge. By late afternoon she would reach the nymph stage, then, and only then, heralded by loud music and running bath water, she would at last venture into the brief world of daylight.

The only exception to this was the day her allowance was paid in. On this day she would generally rouse herself before noon and head for Knightsbridge. By evening, after a suicide dash through the hall with a large Joseph, Kenzo or Katharine Hamnett carrier, which would be hastily spirited upstairs, she would swan around declining dinner in favour of a microwaved Lean Cuisine. Then the metamorphosis would occur. A lot of bath water, loud music and telephone calls would result in this sleek, glossed creature picking its way down the stairs projecting a totally new image to the world. The new outfit would then be worn flat-out to everything until it was referred to as 'that old thing' which 'she wouldn't be seen DEAD in any longer'.

At present, I found this particularly galling since my allowance had been suspended and my dress situation was approaching the terminal stage. Recently, I had even sunk to retrieving some of the despised 'old things' from under Jemima's bed. After a dry clean and a bit of skilful antiquing with the nail scissors they could often be recycled quite successfully.

The trouble was, if they looked anywhere near good on me, Jemima would usually repossess them.

'It's not fair,' I complained to my mother, after a particularly bitter battle over a pair of Pucci leggings. 'You always side with Jemima.'

'Your turn will come,' she said.

A hurtful and inappropriate comment at the best of times.

Once it was clear that Jemima had won the battle over the leggings, I returned to my room fuming about the unfairness of it all. If only Sebastian could see her as she really was.

I opened my well-thumbed *Vogue* at the hallowed 'Sebastian' section. He smiled back at me from the page. A trusting, innocent, adorably male smile. How could anyone so mouthwateringly delicious fall prey to a selfish, vain and extravagant clothes-hog like Jemima? I determined to dedicate what was left of my useful life to saving him from this worthless parasite. It was no more nor less than a plain duty to a fellow human being.

I faced my bedroom mirror with determination. There was very little that a crash diet, a major aerobics drive, a facial, an extended sunbed session, a total hair-restyle and, of course, getting rid of the dreaded railway-tracks couldn't put right.

And then there were my clothes. Suddenly everything I'd ever bought had started to look as if it belonged to someone a year or so younger than me. I rummaged through my wardrobe and the countless fading, shapeless tops and missmatched baggy Hanes bottoms met my gaze. It was going to take a major investment to make any changes in this department.

Which brought me back to my seriously tragic financial situation. My allowance was still suspended and I still owed my mother the £50 I had siphoned off from the Ball ticket money for the haircut. Actually, the Ball ticket situation had now entered its critical final stage.

'Enough is enough, Justine,' Mummy had announced. 'I'm giving those girls until the end of the week, then I really am going to ring their parents.'

What might have seemed like a solution to a less mature and

worldly-wise person than me came unexpectedly in the form of a letter. The letter appeared in a rather curious manner. I found it, addressed to me c/o Mansard Hall, pinned to the school notice board.

I assumed it was some sort of Careers Advice Scheme or Special Offer on Cash's Woven Name Tapes or something, so I threw it into my schoolbag where it sort of mulched down at the bottom with the assorted tissues, leaking cartridges and empty chewing gum packets.

I came across it later that night when I was having a dutiful last ditch search for my lost bus pass.

I tore open the envelope. And read:

Dear Justine,

I thought we ought to keep in touch. I also thought you'd like to know I had some really positive feedback about that last article about you and your friends. Everyone keeps going on about what ravers you must be!

Knowing what a fun person you are, I just wondered if you might have a few more little gems about bright young things high-living in the fast-lane . . . My readers just love to hear about that kind of thing!

Actually—strictly between you and me of course—some papers are willing to pay out good money to people-in-the-know like yourself. If you could provide the right kind of material, naming names, etc . . . we could even be talking about four figures.

Naturally, you'd have the final say on what went into print.

So what have you got to lose?

My contact number is above.

Yours truly (!!!),

   Kathy Kemp

I felt myself go hot all over. The parasite! How dare she! When I thought of what I'd been through!

As it happened the television was on and Juste came through, just as I was positively steaming with fury. Ironically enough, it was in the middle of the Money Programme.

She had her feet up on a desk and was tipping her chair back in the way my mother always said was bound to break one's back not to mention the chair's.

She leaned forward and said:

'Hey there, you look a bit het up about something.'

'I am,' I said and explained about the letter.

'How much did she offer?' asked Juste.

'She wasn't specific. Good money . . . possibly thousands.'

Juste raised an eyebrow and gave a soft whistle, then started tapping at her wrist watch.

'What are you doing . . . ?'

'Hang on, I'm working something out. One or two thou . . . at twelve and a half per cent per annum . . .' she was muttering.

She whistled and then rocked back on her chair again staring at me thoughtfully.

'Disgusting, isn't it!' I said.

Juste shrugged: 'Well, if they're willing to pay . . . let's face it, nobody takes that kind of story seriously anyway.'

'You can't mean you want me to take her up on it?'

'Why not . . . Listen . . .' she said leaning forward and staring at me intently. 'Do you realize how much money that would mean to me now. If you simply went and popped it into a Higher Rate Deposit Account and kind of let it accumulate?'

'How much?'

She checked her watch: 'Could be around ten grand.'

'I don't think I'm hearing this. You want me to go and sell

my soul so that you can get ten measly thousand pounds!?'

'Right now, frankly I could do with the money.'

'You mean you're a bit overdrawn or something?'

'Worse than that . . . positively flat broke.'

This was a blow.

'But surely you must earn money or something?'

'Doing what?' asked Juste.

'Well, I don't know. I've hardly thought about it. I just kind of assumed I'd have a career.'

'Well, you'd better just kind of assume you're resting at the moment,' she said with a yawn.

'So I see,' I said.

'So you will be an angel and think about the offer, won't you?'

'I suppose so . . .'

At that point Juste started fading out.

'Wait!' I said.

But she had gone before I could stop her.

I was left staring at Kathy's letter. Actually, the more I thought about it, I felt it was a bit heavy of Juste to try and sponge off me—a mere child! So with maturity and decisiveness I felt proud of in retrospect, I tore the letter into small pieces and tried to burn it on our 'Real Flame' fire. The ash stayed on the coals for days in small grey accusing flakes.

But that still left *my* money problem. Basically, I could only think of one solution. Well, when my parents had forbidden me to 'see' 'those terrible people' they hadn't mentioned anything about ringing them.

When I called Jason, Franz answered.

'Hi Franz, how are you?'

'Fine,' she said, in a kind of what-in-heaven's-name-is-she-calling-me-for-voice that really got to me.

'Actually I wanted to speak to Jason.'

'I see . . .' she said—like it was a really big deal or something.

'Jason, it's one of your fan club,' I heard her shout.

'Hi!' Jason said mid-chew.

'It's me, Justine.'

'Oh hi! Can't live without me, eh?'

'Look Jason, you know what you said about selling those tickets? I'd love to.'

'Yeh sure, great. Do you want me to drop some round? Er . . . later.'

I thought it might be more tactful to post them to me.

'Just a word of warning though. Don't let them out of your hands until you've actually got the money for them. People simply never pay you back after the event.'

'Do you think I'm stupid or something?' I said.

I put down the receiver with a sigh of relief. Hopefully that was my financial situation somewhat eased. The next thing I had to do was to find a way of dealing with the other great barrier that came between myself and bliss— Jemima.

Hope came in a totally unexpected form. One morning, quite unaccountably, Jemima actually got up and came down in time for breakfast. Mid-way through her third slice of toast, she made an announcement that stunned us into silence.

'I have decided to go Inter-Railing,' said Jemima. 'With Desirée and Candida . . .'

My mother looked dismayed.

'But all those dirty trains, darling, you'll hate it.'

'Nonsense,' said Jemima, delicately extracting the sleeve of her silk pyjamas from the Oxford Marmalade. 'It'll be just too divine to slum it a bit.'

'I think it's a brilliant idea,' I said. (Imagining a whole month of Sebastian all to myself!)

'But anything could happen to three girls alone,' said my mother.

'Nonsense,' said my father. 'It would do her good to have to use a bit of initiative.'

'Just think of all those art galleries and museums and things . . .' I said encouragingly.

'You'll have to economise, you know. I'm not going to pay a fortune for five-star hotels,' he said.

'No hassle,' said Jemima. 'We'll probably sleep on the trains.'

'It all sounds most unsuitable,' said my mother.

'It's not as if she'll be missing much here,' said my father.

'But she will . . . she'll be missing Ascot . . . as well as Wimbledon,' and then she added with a kind of wail '. . . and Henley!'

(It had been a difficult morning for Mummy. She'd had Jane Ponsonby-Haugh on the phone first thing who had mentioned in passing that Fiona had been selected for the Berkeley Dress Show. I knew for a fact it was because another girl had dropped out but it had obviously stung all the same.)

'I haven't got anything to wear for them anyway,' said Jemima.

As far as Daddy was concerned that settled the matter.

From then on the house was full of European Timetables and Jemima's useless friends. They lay around her floor drinking cups of strong black coffee and burning joss-sticks so that my parents couldn't tell they were smoking. In the gaps between the tapes they played I could hear the distant musical names of faraway places bandied around as if they were stops on the London Underground.

At last some sort of schedule was drawn up.

'As far as I can tell you're not going to see anything but the inside of trains and stations,' I commented.

Jemima looked at me witheringly. 'All you've got to remember is to feed my goldfish. And if he's still alive when I
get back you just might get a present.'

Jemima had bought the most enormous rucksack. My
father insisted that she did a trial pack to see if she could get
everything in.

After a couple of hours we were summoned to help her get
it on.

'OK. Let go,' said Jemima. We did and she promptly fell
flat on her back.

A weight check discovered that the packed rucksack
actually weighed almost as much as she did. My father
demanded to see what was inside.

Out came, among other things, her silk pyjamas, a huge
tub of Coconut Body Lotion, a Walkman and about forty
tapes, *my* camera, Daddy's new towelling dressing gown, a
box of Kendal Mint Cake, a jar of Peanut Butter, a crushed
satin evening dress, a pair of Gucci loafers and Samson, her
teddy bear.

'Well, you won't need that for a start,' said our father,
throwing the offending animal across the room.

The morning Jemima left, she tried on the re-packed rucksack in the hall and although she didn't fall over backwards,
she headed out down the hall and through the front door at
some considerable speed.

'And don't talk to strangers!' said my mother, waving
from the door as Daddy drove off with her to Victoria.

I thought talking to strangers was the whole point of Inter-
Railing, but I made no comment.

As Jemima waved through the back window of the Volvo,
I wondered vaguely if this was the last sight I would ever
have of her and if so whether her black satin sheath dress
would automatically be bequeathed to me. I went upstairs to
move *her* stereo into my room. I didn't put a record on

though. I just sat and looked at it and savoured the moment. Peace . . . peace . . . peace . . . for a whole month!

Jemima's goldfish, named Norman after the boy who had given it to her at a fair, had been put into my goldfish bowl to board for the month. (My goldfish was so lacking in personality it had never been given a name.) It was hard to tell whether my goldfish took Norman's presence as a welcome introduction to the pleasures of companionship or an unwarranted intrusion on its privacy. It hovered, gazing out of the bowl, as expressionless as usual. Norman swam around showing off like mad, and then nonchalantly dived through the rock with a hole. I had spent hours patiently trying to train my goldfish to do that!

I sprinkled a little food on the water and Norman shot up in a flash deftly flicking my goldfish out of the way with his tail and gobbled it up. Typical!

My father returned from Victoria, fuming—with the Gucci loafers, the evening dress, the silk pyjamas and Samson under his arm.

The next day I went to school with a light heart. I had packed my make-up bag along with my school books. I was going to make a real effort on the way home. One never knew who one might bump into!

When I entered Fourth Form a subdued little audience was huddled around Leonie's desk. Someone was making sympathetic sounds and Leonie was groping round for a tissue. Six willing hands bearing Kleenex shot out in unison.

'God, what's up, has someone died?' I asked.

Max turned round with a warning frown and said in a stage whisper:

'Sebastian has gone off rock climbing in the French Alps— for a whole month!'

I don't think anyone noticed my face as I tried unsuccessfully to place the French Alps, and judge how close they might be to the main trans-European railway lines, they were all too busy trying to console Leonie.

From then on absolutely nothing worth mentioning happened until after the exams.

13

Actually school was a real pain during that long claustro-phobic summer term. The Pack had well and truly closed ranks and I had been callously cast aside. I had long intense soul-searching sessions wondering about my rating. I realized I hadn't joined the élite status of Leonie and Co. But I certainly hadn't sunk to the level of Non-Descript (not to mention Dreg). In the end, I came to the conclusion I was such an outsider, I simply wasn't rateable at all.

This might have had something to do with the fact that I now went around with Jason. I mean, although we'd always been deeply critical of the Mafia set, they had a kind of sub-versive appeal which I think we all, in our heart of hearts, found hard to resist. Some of this tarnished glamour must have rubbed off on me. I suppose I was simply paying the price of fame. So I just had to keep my head up high and try to live it down. This attitude, of course, was interpreted as pure spoilt-brat arrogance. You can't win, can you?

So, what with Noddy's evil eye on me, and my current status as outcast, Mansard Hall was more or less a no-go area when it came to selling the Energy tickets. But I hit on this absolutely brilliant scheme instead. I found my old junior school telephone list.

I had been sent to this incredibly fashionable junior school where we all wore the most divinely colour-co-ordinated uniforms and spent most of the time in buses learning the geography of inner London. Anyway, my fellow pupils had now been dispersed the length and breadth of England to the cream of the country's boarding schools.

All it took was a single ingeniously-worded letter, photo-stated forty times and sent to their home address with a neat 'Please forward to school' demand to their doting wrinklies.

> *Dear Bodger/Piggy/Tory . . . etc* (it read, as appropriate)
> *Massively missing you — how's life in your far outpost of the social empire? Thought you might be interested in this once-in-a-lifetime, not-to-be-missed social-event-to-start-the-summer-season. Everyone's going to be there . . .* (list of forty names plus brief, if exaggerated, details of event, venue etc.) *Tickets at special offer price through 'Duval Enterprises Inc' before 10 July. Do see how many friends you can bring!*
> *Puddles of pash* (to the girls)
> *Hope to see you there* (to the boys)
> *Justine*

As the term went by I raced down to get the mail each morning, to find among the excruciating vague postcards from Jemima comfortingly fat envelopes containing well-thumbed fivers.

'I'm so glad to see you're keeping up with your old friends,' said my mother, when a particularly large envelope bearing an Eton postmark arrived.

'Umm . . .' I said, ignoring the implied negative reference to my new friends. I was studying a postcard bearing four bleak municipal scenes of Stuttgart.

'*Here we are in Strasbourg,*' went Jemima's message (I

agonised over precisely who 'we' were). '*Everyone seems to speak German here, must be something to do with the Occupation. Weather's lousy and Desirée was sick in her sleeping bag on the Channel crossing so we're having to stay in hotels. Might need extra money, will ring. Luv and kisses—tickle Norman's flippers for me. J.*'

I lifted a couple of plates off the breakfast table and stacked them on the dishwasher. (My parents still hadn't fully recovered from the Grosvenor House scene, so I was slaving away at household chores in a vain attempt to restore my credibility.) Apart from exhausting myself being ostentatiously domesticated, I had found 'studying' was the other effective way to get through to them. I didn't actually study, of course, I just went to my room with the appropriate hangdog face, laid out my books on my desk and played a lot of loud music.

I had become so used to this kind of intensive non-working that I hadn't noticed the end-of-year exams creeping up on me. In fact, according to the date on *The Telegraph* that morning, they were positively looming. So when I had finished a second reading of Jemima's postcard, I stalked through the hall with a sigh, really intending to do some work this time.

My mother was sitting on the sofa with a catalogue of conservatory furniture making calculations on cost and coverings. I hovered in the doorway so that she could get a good view of the books I was carrying. She looked over her glasses.

'Do you think chintz is a bit old hat?' she asked.

'Honestly Mummy, it's up to you. I've got all this to get through.'

'All what?'

'RK revision.'

'Oh my God.'

'How apt.'

'I'll bring you a nice cup of tea up later,' she said, and returned to her catalogue. Tea was considered by Mummy as a kind of balm to all the ills and agonies of exams. It was touching really, she'd generally turn up with a congealing cup of Earl Grey just in time to distract you the very minute you'd settled down.

Before I could start work, however, it seemed absolutely necessary that I should tidy my entire room. This took about two hours and I filled two black plastic rubbish bags with magazines, posters, letters and assorted deeply-moving memorabilia. I placed a clean foolscap pad in the centre of my desk, put a new cartridge into my pen and arranged the reference books in a precise semi-circle around them.

Mummy delivered the cup of Earl Grey and announced she was off to Peter Jones to get some fabric samples, did I want to go with her? Compared with my newly cleared desk, Peter Jones's fabric hall beckoned with a thousand and one delights.

'I can't,' I said with a sigh. 'I simply must get down to it.'

She left with a sympathetic tutting noise.

I took the first book and opened the first page.

The phone didn't ring. No passing hawker conveniently knocked at the front door. No marooned cat mewed helplessly from a neighbouring tree. A force nine gale didn't lift the tiles off the roof. The silence in the house was mind-blowing.

I wandered downstairs and turned on the television.

A model was stalking across some nicely raked desert towards what looked like a bit of polystyrene Grand Canyon. She was joined by a male. As he turned and smouldered across the girl's shoulder, with a technically-impossible-to-survive shock I recognised Sebastian. Those knee-melting green eyes stared through the camera directly into mine.

For some reason I suddenly remembered this phrase from a poem we'd been dissecting in Eng. Lit.—something about 'souls mingling'. In that split second of enlightenment, I understood precisely what it meant.

Over the next four or five commercials, I started to recover. Following the commercial break there appeared to be some sort of health and fitness show. I was about to switch channels when the screen was filled with a woman whom I almost didn't recognise, she was tanned to a deep mahogany colour.

'Justine?'

It was Juste. Her hair was even more vibrantly coloured than usual and she was wearing an over-sized pair of sunglasses. She was lying full-length on some kind of curved bench which I guessed must be a sunbed. She deftly wrapped herself in a towel and slid off the bed staring at me earnestly.

'You look terrible,' she said. 'What's wrong?'

'I'm working,' I said.

'I hope you're not turning into some kind of swot?'

'End of year exams coming up,' I explained.

'Even so,' she said. 'No need to ruin your image.'

She peered through the screen at me with a look of mild horror. 'Hold on a minute . . . you're not getting a *spot* are you.'

'No, I most certainly am not!' I thought I'd been doing a pretty good camouflage job with the Coverstick. It was only a small pimple anyway.

'Well, don't squeeze it. I don't want to erupt in scars.'

'I've got GCSEs next year,' I said trying to get the conversation back on to a higher plane.

She shrugged: 'So who needs qualifications?'

'Everyone!'

'Well, I've managed without.'

I didn't like the sound of this at all.

'No GCSEs?'

'Not a lot.'

'Oh my God.' I grabbed my books and stood up.

'What's up?'

'I'm going back to work.'

'Well mind you don't ruin my eyes—I don't want to wake up one day needing glasses,' said Juste and she climbed back on to the sunbed with a shrug.

I turned off the television and headed back upstairs.

I put in at least two intense hours of study. My mother, brandishing a handful of fabric samples, looked in at one point and then tiptoed away.

'Do you think she's all right?' I heard her whisper to my father on the landing.

'Probably just a phase,' said my father, using his latest expression. He was rather proud of it—it could usefully be applied to practically anything.

I was saved from irreversible brain fatigue by a dreaded familiar ringing on the doorbell.

I craned out of my bedroom window to see Mummy letting in something that closely resembled a bag lady. The end of peace!

I hauled myself to the bannisters. 'Why are you back early?'

Jemima was coming up the stairs dragging her rucksack behind her.

'Thought you might be pining for me,' she said. She left her things on the stairs and threw herself down on my bed.

'God, I don't believe it—a real bed,' she sighed, closing her eyes. Then she opened them again and her gaze fixed on my goldfish bowl.

'Where's Norman?' she demanded.

'He's . . . out,' I said.

'Goldfish can't be OUT,' said Jemima. 'Where is he?'

I searched for a gentle way to break the news that I had had to flush him down the loo.

'He had a sailor's burial,' I said.

Jemima looked suitably grief-stricken.

'Honestly, I did all I could. He just went all sort of lop-sided. So I put him into intensive care in my washbasin and he swam endlessly clockwise round and round until the next morning when I found him floating on the top.'

'Well, that saves the argument about the pressie anyway,' she said in a practical manner. 'I ran out of money so I didn't get you anything.'

'It's the thought that counts,' I said. 'Did you have a good time?'

'Don't ask,' she said. 'I spent most of the time zipped up over my head in my sleeping bag to ward off marauders. Desirée kept me alive by stuffing *baguettes* in the top. The only impression I really got of Europe was the difference in the flavour of the ham in the middle.'

'Didn't you meet anyone—exciting?' I probed.

'Not wildly.'

'No dazzling males?' I probed further.

'Only German boys with incredibly hairy knees who kept producing guitars and singing Bob Dylan songs.'

'No one we know?' I asked.

'Shouldn't you be at school?' she said and yawned.

'Study leave,' I said. 'I'm in the middle of exams.'

But she'd wandered out of the room. I shouldn't have expected sympathy. All that sort of thing was now buried in Jemima's distant past.

I was left wondering how deep and devious Jemima was being. In my bones I knew she must have met up with Sebastian. I didn't get at the truth until much later that day. That evening, I just happened to be sitting on the stairs painting my toe nails after my bath while Jemima was on the phone.

'Hi . . .' (muffled scream) '. . . Yes Me!'

'. . . (muffled scream in response)' It was evidently a girl-friend.

'Dreadful! I lost them in Paris because they were being *such* a drag.'

'. . . . .'

'Briefly.'

'. . . . .'

'Well, after positively spending a fortune on international telephone calls, we actually met.'

'. . . . .'

'In Geneva, when I was on my way back . . . at least, I think it was Geneva. God he was looking divine.'

I smudged my nail varnish at that point.

'It was terribly poignantly *Brief Encounter*,' Jemima continued in a lowered voice. 'I had just ten minutes before my train left for Lyons and he was heading back to some ghastly base camp half way up the mountain. I lent him my neck cushion so I got a crick in my neck all the way back. I doused it with Coco—I thought that might get through to him, you know like people learn French in their sleep?'

'. . . . .'

'Well, he's bound to. He's got to return it, hasn't he?'

'. . . . .'

I sensed that the conversation was coming to a close so I leaped into the bathroom and turned on the taps and missed the rest.

About a week later, Leonie came into school positively radiating delight. She threw herself with abandon into a chair and put her feet up on my desk.

'Guess what?' she said and a crowd of eager Dregs

gathered round obediently trying to.

'He's back.'

'How do you know?' demanded Henry.

'I rang his home, his mother said he got back yesterday.'

'Have you seen him?' asked a Dreg, breathlessly.

'Not yet, but he's bound to call me tonight,' said Leonie.

Huh I thought, but diplomatically I said nothing.

On the way home that night I dropped into Boots. They had quite a stock of blue-covered neck cushions like Jemima's. I bought one and hovered by the perfumery counter. While the assistant wasn't looking I sprayed it with the Coco tester.

When I got home, I found Jemima curled up in front of the television.

'Honestly,' she said, 'you might have recorded "Neighbours" for me while I was away. I've totally lost the thread.'

'By the way,' I said, 'I've got something for you.'

I took the carefully crumpled cushion out of my schoolbag.

Jemima looked fraught.

'Where did you get it?' she asked.

'From Leonie. Apparently Sebastian got back last night,' I said. 'You didn't tell me you met him.'

'You didn't ask,' she said, acidly.

She went upstairs without seeing the end of 'Neighbours' and I could hear her banging drawers in her room, evidently dressing to go out. Half an hour later she came down and announced she was meeting someone called Vincent in Oriel and could I take any phone messages for her.

I waited for the expected phone call.

It came at around 9 p.m.

'Hello . . . is Jemima in?'

It was such ages since I'd spoken to him my voice went all thick and husky.

'Hallo,' I kind of growled.

'Who's that?'

'Justine,' I said, clearing my throat.

'Oh hi, it's Sebastian. Do you know where she is?'

'Yes, she's gone out with Vincent,' I said.

'I see . . .' he said. 'Do you know when she'll be back?'

'Late,' I said. 'Very late. If at all.'

'I see . . .' he said.

'If it's about the neck cushion,' I said helpfully, 'she's got a new one. She said not to worry, you can keep it.'

'Right . . .' he said. 'Could you tell her I called?'

'Of course.'

'Don't forget now.'

'I won't.'

It would be just too seriously heart-rending to describe the agonising sensations involved in the relationship I was developing with Sebastian. It's the kind of thing no-one, simply no-one, could understand unless they'd been through it themselves. The whole thing was made so much more utterly poignant by his total ignorance of the situation.

14

It was just one of those flukes of fate that Jemima should have
met Vincent. Vincent (pronounced *Vin Cent*, as in French)
was born in Paris some (he claims) thirty or so years ago, and
works as a freelance photographer. Anyway, as luck would
have it, Vincent discovered Jemima's true vocation. She was
born to be a photographic model. It should have been
obvious to us all from the very beginning. Let's face it, the
only things Jemima really has a talent for are making herself
look sickeningly stunning and sitting around doing absolutely nothing.

'Vincent is a total darling. He says he'll produce my Composite for me,' said Jemima when she returned later that
night to disrupt a family dinner.

'What's a Composite?'

Jemima answered, pitying my ignorance. 'A Composite is
a set of pictures in different poses, which one has to have in
order to get modelling work.'

She helped herself to what was left of the fricassée.

'Modelling!' I said. (If there was one thing that was going
to throw her into the path—and arms—of Sebastian, it was
modelling.) 'How indescribably naff.'

The family ignored this comment and continued talking as

if I were part of the furniture.

'But we've got masses of lovely snaps of you,' said Mummy.

'Honestly, you've no idea. You have to have professional pictures,' said Jemima.

'So that they can retouch all the zits and bulges,' I added, giving her an extra helping of pudding.

Jemima gave me a withering look.

So that was that. After spending an absolute fortune on pampering her body and several long photographic sessions with Vincent, Jemima's Composite arrived—together with an enormous bill.

'He didn't say anything about charging for it,' said Jemima.

'I don't expect you asked,' commented my father as he signed the cheque.

'Don't worry, I'll pay you back. I'm bound to get work soon,' said Jemima.

'I'll believe that when you get your first job,' said my father.

But, to everyone's amazement, Jemima did get work. She was almost instantly signed up with Zoom of Covent Garden which, according to her, was the very best model agency in town. It also happened to be the one that Sebastian was with.

I now considered that Jemima was in danger of acute, if not terminal, vanity. But actually I was wrong. Coming into direct competition with loads of girls, many of whom were better looking, actually brought on a total reappraisal of her looks.

'Everyone there is so incredible,' wailed Jemima. 'I'm sure I'll never get work. Even the receptionist is stunning.' And she mooned around having a mega-confidence crisis which, if anything, was worse than vanity.

But apparently, Jemima had what they called 'today's

look'. She could pout into the camera with that particular expression that our family had always called her 'Spoilt Brat' face and shot after shot came out looking one hell of a lot better than she did in real life.

Fiona, Zoom's (stunning) receptionist was constantly on the phone and the S-B face started to appear in various publications. People stopped me on the stairs at school to point out that they'd seen my sister in this or that magazine. It was all getting heartily nauseating.

Mummy revelled in it. She cut out all the pictures and kept them in a loose-leaf file and brought them out in a really cringe-making way when her Conservative Bring-and-Buy group met.

And then one evening Jemima wafted into my room and announced:

'Guess what, I've got an audition for a commercial tomorrow, with guess who?'

'Who?' I asked, but I didn't have to guess.

'Sebastian,' she sighed.

Once alone again I considered the implications of the situation. A commercial would throw the two of them together for days and days. On the one hand this could mean that Sebastian would have the time to discover what a useless, worthless creature Jemima actually was. On the other, Jemima could be 'so-sickeningly-nice' when she tried. Anyone as touchingly male and vulnerable as Sebastian would be bound to be taken in by her. This required drastic action!

I had to consult Juste!

After waiting an absolute eternity for Juste to make an appearance, she at last came through, just before eleven o'clock after Daddy had sent me to bed for the second time.

'For God's sake think of something fast!' said Juste when I explained about the commercial.

'Like what!' I said.

'Anything!' said Juste. 'If those two get together I'm telling you, that'll be it!'

'It?'

'Yes . . . IT.'

'So what do you suggest?'

'I don't know . . . use your ingenuity. Put laxatives in her coffee, cut her hair off in her sleep, burn all her shoes! Anything!'

'Honestly Juste!'

My father's head appeared round the door.

'And get off the phone, this minute!' he said.

'I'm not on the phone, Daddy,' I said as I docilely turned off the television and made for bed.

The next day, the day of the audition, I answered the front door to find a huge bunch of roses being delivered. There was a small envelope pinned to it, addressed to Jemima. I tore open the envelope and put it in my pocket. The card inside simply said with devastating originality:

'To the most beautiful girl in the world.
All my love—Sebastian.'

I stood in the hall for a moment holding the bunch of roses. I could hear noises above. Jemima was about to come downstairs. She had been simply hours getting ready and insisted I ordered a cab to the model agency.

'*All* my love!'

The doorbell rang again.

It was the cab driver.

'Cab for Covent Garden?' he said, providing unconscious inspiration.

'Yes,' I said. 'Can you deliver these please.'

I pinned the card back on the bunch of roses and directed him to hand them over to Fiona at Zoom.

Ten minutes later, Jemima wafted downstairs.

'Hasn't my cab come?' she asked.

I shook my head.

'Damn, I'll be late. I'll have to take pot luck and hail one.'

With that she shot out of the front door.

At lunch-time Jemima arrived home demanding lunch and looking decidedly miffed.

'Did you get it?'

'I don't know yet,' she said. 'I can't stand that Fiona woman, she treats you like dirt and she's only a bloody receptionist.' She dug forcefully into her salad and spiked a radish.

Contentedly, I pictured the roses prominently displayed on Fiona's desk.

Later that day I arrived back from tennis coaching to find Jemima on the phone. I lingered in the hall taking off my tennis shoes.

'What do you mean you didn't send them. I saw them with my own eyes.'

'. . . . . .'

'Don't lie to me.'

'. . . . .'

'Yes, you are. Anyway, I can see by the way she looks at you.'

'. . . . .'

'You're just saying that.'

'. . . . .'

138

'Well, I'll need a lot of convincing.'

'. . . . .'

'Tonight?'

One thing nobody ever tells you, so you have to find out slowly and painfully for yourself, is that love thrives on discord.

15

The curious thing was, though it didn't strike me until it happened, I had never actually had a conversation with Sebastian—face to face that is. I'd planned and planned just how incredibly cool I would be when we at last got some time alone together. But these things are not always perfectly timed.

Jemima was busy in the bathroom when the doorbell rang.

'KNICKERS! What's the time?!'

'Nine-thirty.'

'That must be Sebastian. Go and let him in.'

'Mummy'll kill you.'

'She can't, can she? She's out. Be an angel and keep him entertained. He can't see me looking like this!'

Jemima, as usual, had not so much as an eyelash out of place.

I had odd blobs of Coverstick on my face where I was doing another hasty camouflage job. I was also in my dressing gown and woolly slippers.

'What about me?'

'Oh, he won't care what *you* look like,' said Jemima.

The doorbell rang again and Jemima bolted into her bedroom and locked the door.

I dragged a comb through my hair and splashed some foundation on my face.

The doorbell rang a third time, more urgently. I flew downstairs and opened the door.

He was standing on the doorstep looking absolutely scrummy, in fact, virtually edible. The conversation that followed isn't exactly going to go down in history.

'Is Jemima in?'

'Yes, she is.'

'Can I come in?'

'Yes, of course.'

'Good.'

At that point he noticed the hall mirror. He cast an appreciative glance at himself and leaned forward to rearrange, by at least a millimetre, a strand of perfectly gelled hair.

'Jemima should be down soon.'

This statement was almost immediately contradicted by the sound of bath water running upstairs.

'Perhaps you'd better come and sit down.'

He seemed reluctant to drag himself away from the mirror.

'Would you like a drink or something?'

He gave himself one last sideways glance, trying to catch himself in profile, then followed me into the sitting room.

'We've got all the usual things. Gin, whisky, vodka, sherry, etc. That's if Jemima hasn't been bingeing through the drinks cupboard again.' I caught a glimpse of Sebastian's suitably shocked face.

'Orange juice would be fine. With ice, a lot of ice,' he said.

I shuffled off to the kitchen and brought back an orange juice with ice . . . a lot of it.

Sebastian had carefully arranged himself on the sofa, one arm thrown casually over the back.

I avoided the sofa and sat down opposite him. It was a bad

choice of position. I was feeling hot and flustered under my Coverstick. I tried to kind of fold my slippers out of sight under the chair.

'Jemima shouldn't be long.'

'She knows I'm here?'

'Yes.'

It was at that point the telephone rang. It was Chuck.

'Oh hello,' I said. 'No, sorry she's in the bath.'

Justine, what the hell's going on,' said Chuck.

'No, I don't think she can tonight, she's going out . . .' I said.

Sebastian tried to look as though he wasn't listening.

'I'm sure she'd love to . . . I'll tell her you called. See you on Sunday as usual,' I said.

'Who was that?' asked Sebastian.

'Vincent, a friend of Jemima's.' I raised an eyebrow meaningfully. 'Would you like some more orange juice?'

'No, that was fine,' he said rather fast.

Another couple more centuries of silence passed.

I was starting to wish we had a cat or something to provide some form of distraction.

'You wouldn't like to run upstairs and sort of hurry her up, would you?' he said.

I made my way upstairs, in my own good time, and shouted through the locked bathroom door: 'For God's sake hurry up! I'm practically having to get out the family photo album.'

Jemima's head appeared. She had a green face mask on.

'Don't hassle me. I'm hurrying,' she said between clenched lips.

On the way downstairs the phone rang again.

This time it was Jason.

'How many tickets have you sold?'

'About thirty I think, why?'

'If we don't get the numbers up, we're going to have to cancel.'

(This was serious, man. I had already given my mother fifty pounds of the money I had received so far to pay her back the famous Ball ticket money. 'And about time too,' she had said, very ungratefully I thought.)

'What do you suggest I do?' I asked.

'Have a major blitz, ring round everyone and say the tickets are running out, so they'll have to come up with the cash fast.'

'OK,' I said, putting my hand over the receiver. 'I'll tell her. And she loved the perfume by the way. Coco is her favourite.'

Then I hung up.

When I regained the sitting room, I found Sebastian hovering near the door. He had discovered the mirror over the fireplace and was checking up on the gleaming perfection of his teeth.

He shot back on to the sofa pretty quickly. I could see he was dying to know who the call was from, so I put him out of his misery by saying casually:

'I wish Jemima would answer the phone to some of these people. That was the third time Jean-Pierre's called.'

Sebastian made a sort of non-committal grunting noise and slumped down on the sofa.

'Shall we watch television?' he suggested. He switched it on before I had a chance to reply. It was a 1940s black and white movie.

As I dreaded, with the merest imperceptible electronic fizz, Juste slipped into the heroine's place. She wasn't going to miss out on a scene like this. She stared straight out of the screen and took in a totally false impression of the situation. She raised an eyebrow.

I've no idea what the movie was, but it was something

deeply melodramatic and we'd arrived at one of those really cringe-worthy bits where the hero and heroine are having the meaningful heartfelt conversation where all is revealed:

'. . . *Can't you see, she's not worthy of you* . . .' Juste sighed into the camera.

She was making a real exhibition of herself, over-acting like mad.

'*One day you'll realize . . . from the day we were born . . . we were destined for each other . . .*'

'That woman reminds me of someone,' said Sebastian.

'Does she?' I could hardly trust myself to speak. I could feel an ultra-serious mega-blush coming on.

'Who the hell does she remind me of?' said Sebastian to himself.

The situation was saved by Jemima.

'Darling . . .' she wafted into the room in a cloud of Coco and the miniest gold mini-skirt. All attention was automatically diverted from the television.

There was a lot of kissing on both cheeks and mutual admiration and the two of them swept out through the hall, each casting a last long loving look at themselves in the mirror.

As the door slammed, I turned to Juste.

'That was really embarrassing,' I said.

'I was only trying to help,' said Juste.

'I don't need that kind of help, thank you,' I said.

'Basically, I think you're letting him slip through your fingers. You're not even trying. And anyway, let's face it, you're going about the whole thing in totally the wrong way,' said Juste.

'What do you mean?'

'What you're forgetting is that men love nothing better than a real challenge. Brings out the animal in them.'

'You mean he just thinks Jemima's playing hard to get?'

'Precisely. You'd be much better off getting her to smother him in passionate possessiveness.'

'How on earth do I do that? You know as well as I do, there's basically only one person Jemima cares passionately about—herself.'

'Well you'll have to think of something—and fast,' said Juste. 'Remember it's your future at stake.'

And she faded herself out.

I switched the television off.

Boy, had I got problems! I decided to tackle them one at a time. I spent the rest of the evening on the phone. You won't believe what a hassle it is to get through to anyone at boarding school.

At Lady Charlotte's, I was put through to the Fourth Form dormitory where a girl answered.

'Could I speak to Chrissie Hampshire, please?'

'Oh yah fine, hang on . . .'

And I was left hanging, to the distant boarding-school sounds of muffled screams, footsteps, water running and a concert of stereos. After ten minutes of unsuccessfully shouting and whistling down the phone, I gave up.

At Wolde, where I tried to get through to a couple of the boys, I was put through to the bursar's office.

'No, I'm afraid you can't speak to the boys, unless it's an emergency of course. They can only call out.'

'But this is an emergency,' I said.

'May I know the nature of the problem?'

'It's kind of a financial emergency.'

'Could you tell me who's calling please?'

I considered for a moment whether the name Justine Duval would mean anything to this woman, and then I rang off.

By midnight, I had only managed to get through to one girl at Windlesham and she only wanted two measly tickets. I decided to call it a day and go to bed.

That's when Chuck managed to get through.

'Hi Justine—you running a phone-in chat-line or something?'

'Had trouble getting through?'

'Not really, though I think I might need physio on my dialling finger. What's all this stuff you were giving me on the phone earlier?'

'Far too complicated to explain . . .' I said truthfully. 'Was it anything in particular you were calling for?'

'Well, actually I was going to give you the opportunity of the night out of a lifetime.'

'Oh really?'

'Well, not really—the end-of-term school dance actually.'

'Oh really.'

'Look, honestly Justine, if I could think of anyone else to invite, I would.'

'Go on, dole out the flattery—I'm listening.'

'Frankly, I'm desperate.'

'What about the girls at school?'

'Only the "difficult to place" items left.'

'What about Franz?'

'Still recovering from the bathroom drama.'

'OK. When is it then?'

It just so happened that it fell on the same Saturday as the Energy party.

'No sorry, I'm tied up that night anyway.'

'Curses. I was counting on you.'

Just at that moment it occurred to me that I was going to need a suitably legitimate excuse to get out of the house that night.

'On second thoughts . . . I might be able to shift things round a bit.'

'You could?'

'I'll do my best.'

'I knew I could rely on you.'

'I know,' I said guiltily. I was going to have to think of something drastic to let myself out without injuring his male pride—but the dance was yonks away, anyway.

16

The next morning I hovered around the house until Jemima emerged at last—at one o'clock—for breakfast.

'Did you have a good time?' I asked.

Jemima yawned: 'When?'

'Last night.'

'Oh last night. It was a bit of a bore really.' She started reading her horoscope in my *Just Seventeen*.

'What did you do?' I prompted.

'Oh, nothing much.'

'Till five in the morning?'

'Oh, if you must know, we went for a drink and met these people who said to come on to Jasper's because they were having a massive party, but it was full of really daggy people so we took in a few clubs and had a meal at Up All Night and then someone mentioned the Stars and Stripes Ball, so I borrowed a ghastly skirt thing off some girl whose flat we'd ended up in and we all piled into Geoff's car and gatecrashed. It was all a bit tedious really.'

It sounded like one hell of a way to get bored to me.

'What happened to Sebastian?'

'Oh him. I lost him somewhere. He was being an absolute drag anyway. He kept chatting up other girls.'

Jemima had put down the magazine and was digging into her Special K.

I picked it up and the sight of the Problem Page suddenly gave me an idea . . .

'Listen to this . . .' I said. 'My boyfriend doesn't take enough notice of me (I improvised). I love him very much but he's always eyeing up other women. What should I do?'

I switched to a mature caring voice: 'Show him how you feel. Buy him a present or cook him a meal. It's probably a cry for attention—all he needs is reassurance.'

'Huh . . .' said Jemima, mid-spoonful. 'He'll be lucky.'

At that point the phone rang.

'Justine?'

'Is it for me?' Jemima asked expectantly. I shook my head and she swept with injured dignity out of the room.

'Yes?'

'It's Piggy . . . Look I can't talk long. I'm in a call box. It's about those tickets. Have you got any left?'

'A few . . .' I said, visualising the pile in the drawer.

'I need thirty at least. Thirty or thirty-two . . . Not sure yet.'

'I might be able to manage that.'

'Can you send them to this friend of mine at Wolde?'

'I absolutely never let people have tickets till I get the money.'

'But he says no-one will part with the money till they get the tickets.'

'I'll have to pay for those tickets myself if I don't get the money back,' I said. 'How do you know they'll pay up?'

'Look, he's a really good friend of mine,' said Piggy. 'He won't let you down.'

We argued a bit longer and I could see the prospect of £450 receding fast. And, *more seriously*, I could also see the deep dire threat of the whole thing being cancelled.

'Look,' said Piggy. 'What if I get him to deliver the money to you in person?'

It seemed Simon (the friend from Wolde) was coming to London on the day of the party. I tried to work out the commission in my head—anyway, commission on around thirty tickets must amount to a nice round sum. It was cutting it a bit fine having the money delivered on the day of the party, though.

Finally Piggy said: 'If anything goes wrong, I'll pay you back myself.'

So I agreed, against my better judgement. I just managed to get down the details of Simon's surname and house, etc before Piggy ran out of money. Then I raced upstairs and put thirty tickets in an envelope, addressed it and flew down to catch the mid-morning post.

The thought of all that money made me positively ache to spend it. I decided to dip into the funds I had so far and invest in something 'seriously flared' in Harrods' Summer Sale. I was making my way through to Way In when I came across Jemima in the Men's Department. She was standing in a sort of trance, staring at the rows of designer silk ties. These were ferociously expensive and Jemima simply never spends any money on anyone but herself.

'Buying a present for Daddy?' I asked. I don't think she actually caught the note of irony in my voice.

'Do you think Sebastian would look good in this?' Jemima asked, holding out a Cerruti number.

'He probably would if you left the price tag on,' I commented. 'He'd be flattered at any rate.'

'You don't think it's too obvious?' said Jemima.

'Too obviously what?'

'Too obviously . . . obvious,' she said.

'It's only a tie, not a condom,' I said.

Jemima actually blushed. Do you know, in point of fact, I can't ever remember seeing Jemima blush before.

That's when I realised that this was IT.

I had to go and stand in the Food Hall for about ten minutes while I regained my composure. I just stood there staring at the wet fish display. It's a pretty depressing sight at the best of times, but today the fish all seemed to stare back at me with a particularly doleful expression. They reminded me of Norman.

No-one who hasn't gone through a deep and tragically moving love affair (preferably when the object of their devotion wilfully ignores their existence and falls prey to their worthless sister) can possibly understand how seriously suicidal I felt.

So I bought myself a full quarter pound of American Jelly Beans to cheer myself up. But I hadn't the heart to eat them—not even the Blueberry ones.

In fact, the sight of all those Sale shoppers busily battling for bargains I was missing had a profoundly distressing effect on me. I decided to give Way In a miss and made my way home through the crowds of frantic panic buyers.

To cap it all, when I got back home there was a message for Jemima to ring Fiona. She had landed the part in the commercial.

'You won't believe this,' said Jemima. She had arrived back weighed down by Chanel Boutique carrier bags and flown to the phone.

She was now standing poised with her hand cupped over the receiver.

'Sebastian's in it too. And they're going to shoot in Paris!'

'When?'

'Some time next week.' Then she added casually so that Fiona, on the other end, couldn't help hearing: 'We'll probably leave early on Saturday so we can start with a restful weekend.'

'But you can't,' I pointed out when she'd rung off. 'You're meant to be looking after me.'

'Then you'll just have to keep quiet about it, won't you,' said Jemima.

That was the weekend when I was in grave danger of being carted off to Trudgings with the Oldies. It was also the weekend of the Energy thrash and I had begged for permission to stay in London with the excuse that I shouldn't miss going to the nice 'suitable' end-of-term school dance with Chuck. The Oldies had (I suspect to prove how un-class-conscious they were) grudgingly agreed to let me stay, as long as Jemima kept an eye on me.

When Saturday morning came Mummy had left us enough food for a siege. Daddy had gone on and on about barricading all the doors and windows and double-locking and how not to forget to operate the burglar alarm. At last we stood on the doorstep waving goodbye to the receding Volvo with expressions of fixed sweetness-and-innocence.

'Right,' said Jemima as the car turned the corner and she shot upstairs.

I followed her at a distance.

Jemima's room greeted me with its usual elegant disarray. Silk pyjamas draped to shade the table lamp. Open magazines all over the floor. And her bedside table laid out like a shrine displaying her latest collection of trophies: roses (not just distressed but frankly deceased); assorted postcards; a bottle of Fendi half unwrapped with its gift tag prominently displayed; and a collection of invitations neatly fanned out but no doubt not replied to.

On the bed lay a brand new Louis Vuitton suitcase, open and half-packed.

'What are you doing?' I said.

'Isn't it obvious?' said Jemima.

'Mummy'll have a blue fit!'

'She won't know, will she?' said Jemima.

With that she disappeared into the bathroom and started to throw things into a sponge bag.

I delved into the suitcase and was reclaiming my blusher brush, hair gel, lip salve, Gold Spot and a couple of hairbands when I noticed a small packet. It was The Pill. This was the final straw.

I slipped the pack into my pocket. Jemima was still in the bathroom noisily sorting through her arsenal of make-up bottles.

'Be an angel and find me a hairband. I've got to meet Sebastian at Heathrow at midday,' I heard Jemima shout as I slid out of her room and locked the door. I glided down a flight and locked another. As I mentioned earlier, Daddy keeps the whole place like Fort Knox. All the internal doors have locks. By the time I had double-locked the front door there were no less than three solid locked doors between Jemima and the outside world.

Then I went to the nearest phone box and rang Jason on the Mafia car phone.

'Hi Jason. Can you still give me a lift tonight?'

'Hi Gorgeous, sure. I'll come and pick you up.' (Loud interference.)

'No look, can you pick me up from Sloane Square?'

'OK. Wait by the Monument. I'll pick you up at nine.' (More loud interference.)

I spent the afternoon lurking in Harrods. Every department

had its own particular brand of nostalgia. And every one re-minded me of Jemima. There was the Children's Shoe Department where we had haggled with Mummy over Start-Rites versus Penny Loafers. And the Pet Department where we had once saved up together and bought a white rabbit and then taken it back after three days because it was *so boring*. And there was the Men's Department where Jemima had bought Sebastian that mega-bucks tie. Apparently, he'd been quite pleased with it. He said it went with his eyes.

I wondered with deep pangs of empathy how long he'd waited at Heathrow. Surely, being let down like that would once and for all make him see Jemima as she really was.

I was just hovering in the TV Department watching car-toons to kill time when I heard this 'Pssst . . .' from behind.

From inside a deeply lacquered inlaid rosewood cabinet, Juste's face appeared on the screen. She looked terrible!

'I've got to speak to you . . .' she hissed.

'Not now . . .' I whispered. 'There are masses of people around.'

'Listen . . . I'm in deep trouble. SBITE are on to me!'

She looked frantic, wild-eyed with her hair all over the place. 'Have you got that money yet?'

'What money? And who the hell are SBITE?'

'Police!' she hissed. 'Special-Branch-Illegal-Telecommuni-cation-Emissions. They must have tracked down our wave-length. I can't talk long. I've had a summons.'

An assistant in a dark suit was watching me suspiciously. I suppose it wasn't every day he spotted a fourteen-year-old girl talking to his televisions.

'Look, basically it's all your fault,' said Juste. 'It's going to mean a vast fine. You've got to get me some money. If I can't pay . . .' her voice faltered.

'What?'

'Holloway . . .'

'Oh my God!' I said.

The assistant was bearing down on me.

'Were you particularly interested in the rosewood?' he asked in a supercilious tone.

I hurriedly slammed the doors of the cabinet, shutting in the ghastly vision of Juste.

'. . . It is also available in mahogany.'

'Actually, I'm after walnut,' I said. 'To match my cocktail cabinet.'

'Pity . . .' he said. 'It doesn't come in walnut.'

When Harrods closed I took refuge in the Chelsea Cannon and had to sit through the early performance of an excruciatingly boring PG film. The cinema was full of out-of-practice Daddies simply stuffing their children with chocolate and popcorn. Half-way through a girl two rows in front of me got up and for a split second, outlined against the screen, it looked like Jemima, but of course it wasn't.

By the time I got to Sloane Square I was having a real attack of paranoia. I kept imagining I could hear loud bellowings and crashing noises coming from the direction of Cheyne Walk. I wasn't quite sure whether to feel virtuous or guilty. After all, I rationalised, Mummy would fully approve . . . On the other hand, I wondered if Jemima would ever speak to me again, and decided most probably not.

I just prayed that Jason wouldn't be late: the sooner I got out of London the better. Several times I actually visualised Jemima appearing like an angel of vengeance out of the traffic. I strained my eyes into the distance trying to discern the approaching Mafia car.

On any ordinary day, it would have stood out from the general run of traffic like a slice of strawberry in a school fruit salad, but it just so happened that tonight was the last Saturday of the month—'cruising night'. Virtually every second car was a pink Cadillac with vast tail-fins.

Sleek limousines slid by offering glimpses of leopard-skin seating and deliciously posey people in their deliciously posey clothes. A Marilyn look-alike gave me a regal wave from the back of a white Cadillac convertible. And a fake James Dean actually hooted at me.

Then, between these visions, the sight of Piggy brought me down to earth.

He was weaving his way through the cars carrying a can of lager.

'Piggy!'

That instant, I remembered with renewed panic that I'd left before Simon had delivered the ticket money.

He spun round and caught sight of me.

'Justine!'

'Am I glad to see you! That Simon guy hasn't shown up with the money.'

'Hasn't he?'

'Are you sure you gave him the right address?'

'I said it was Cheyne Walk, I wasn't sure of the number.'

'It's 122.'

'I assumed you'd put a note or something in with the tickets.'

I shook my head.

'Oh dear,' said Piggy. 'I'd better ring him.'

'You can't. They won't take in-coming calls at the school.'

'Oh dear,' said Piggy again.

'Do you realize I'm going to have to pay for all those tickets out of my own pocket if I don't get the money!'

'Don't worry,' said Piggy. 'I'll think of something.'

But what? I wondered. Was he going to 'blaze' all the lampposts from Sloane Square Tube?

Before I could enquire further, he lurched off into the traffic once more.

'See you at the party!' He waved his can of lager and

drenched a passing yuppie in an open-topped BMW.

My heart sank. My four hundred and fifty pounds . . . I was highly unlikely to see it now. I was never going to be able to bank it for Juste. And more to the point, I was never going to be able to pay it back!

Jason *was* late of course. I had to loiter for about an hour by the Monument feeling really conspicuous.

Then, at last, the Mafia car drove up.

Jason flung open the door.

'Come on, slide your gorgeous body over my way,' he said.

So I did.

17

We had a bit of trouble actually getting out of London. We were forced over Battersea Bridge and back over Chelsea Bridge three times before we extricated ourselves from the bonnet-to-tail line of Cruisers.

In the car, besides Jason, there was a boy who said his name was Andrew. He was short and dark with ferocious side-burns and a manic handshake. He kept getting enormously het-up about the traffic jam and leaned out of the window trying to persuade people to let us through the way we wanted to go—which was mainly over pavements and the wrong way round roundabouts.

At last we broke free and zoomed full-throttle out towards the M4. There wasn't much traffic at that time of night and as we clocked up reassuring miles between Jemima and myself, I couldn't help noticing that the hand on the speedometer went round to numbers Daddy's car would never dream of doing.

Somewhere outside Windsor the traffic started to build up and that was when I realized with a stomach-turning jolt that I had totally forgotten to let Chuck know that I wasn't going to turn up at the dance. I had this agonising vision of him standing, limp and helpless, outside North Thames

Comprehensive for the entire night. I sat miserably gazing out of the window having a mega-attack of guilt.

Jason had started to get very agitated about the traffic. He kept switching lanes quite unnecessarily, it wasn't getting us any further. Then as we slowed down to around five miles an hour, I noticed that cars were stopped at all sorts of odd angles on the grass verge.

'This must be it,' said Jason.

There were policemen up ahead with torches. As we drew level, one of them shone a torch into the car and eyed us up and down.

'Keep moving,' he said. 'You can't stop here. The whole thing's been cancelled.'

'Take no notice,' said Jason in an undertone. 'They always try that. Shout if you see a gap big enough to dump the car in.'

We crawled on for about another mile until at last the car lurched off the road and skidded to a halt on the muddy verge.

We all climbed out.

'Do we need tickets?' I said, suddenly realizing I'd left mine at home. 'Am I going to get in without one?'

'Wear this,' said Andrew. He handed me a badge with 'Organiser' rather roughly photostated on it. I noticed they were both wearing them.

'Who needs tickets? Not when you're in the company of yours truly. This way, *mesdames et messieurs.*'

And he set off at a trot along the hard shoulder. We followed until we saw lights in the distance and Andrew headed off the road.

We caught up to find him stretching a gap in a barbed wire fence.

'After you,' he said. And I climbed through.

We trudged up a steeply sloping field and as we reached the

crest the sound hit us like the blast from an atomic explosion.

It must be deafening inside, I thought, as we looked down on a vast marquee.

At the entrance a bouncer stopped us.

'Tickets?'

'We're the management,' said Jason.

'You're the fifth bunch of management I've had through tonight. I'm not letting anyone in till I see a proper ticket. That's my orders.'

'Look, if you'd let me past, I could find someone who'll vouch for us,' said Jason.

'So could I,' said Andrew, slipping behind the bouncer.

'Hey, watch it,' said the man, swinging round and catching Andrew and virtually lifting him off the ground.

'Move!' said Jason and gave me a huge shove and we found ourselves inside.

It didn't take a minute to lose ourselves in the crowd. By the time the bouncer realized what had happened we had disappeared into the thick cloud of smoke and coloured ice vapour.

'I can smell strawberries,' I said.

'Strawberry smoke,' said Jason. 'It's meant to turn you on.'

'Does it?'

'I don't think so. But let me know if it does!'

As we got nearer the speakers I shouted in Jason's ear. 'What about Andrew?'

'He'll find a way in,' he replied.

We squeezed our way through the mass of seething bodies.

'Sorry,' I said as a totally spaced-out boy lurched into me.

'No sweat,' he said and continued dancing without even opening his eyes.

I soon began to realize why. It was the music. It was a kind of very, very loud Rap, blasting out the same beat, after beat, after beat . . .

Andrew joined us.

'How did you get in?' said Jason.

'Through the Ladies,' said Andrew. 'Caused a bit of a stir.'

To start with, I think I was dancing in a kind of loose group with Jason and Andrew. I can't remember quite when I lost sight of them. It didn't seem to matter at the time. Nothing did.

Laser lights, Day-Glo-pink smoke and the clash of psyche-delic clothes mixed in a dazzling slur: luminous biker shorts, juicy jungle prints, muddled, tie-dyed, tasteless, ripped, hanging-loose, skinned-alive-tight—anything as long as it could definitely not be categorised! In my black gear I felt like a London pigeon that had made a forced landing in the Parrot House.

Needless to say, nobody, absolutely nobody, was taking any notice of me. But I could hardly take this personally as actually, no-one was taking any notice of anyone. There was a total lack of body contact or any communication whatsoever.

We were caught up in the music. Seriously, it was pretty unreal. I got this odd sense we were all part of the same big warm throbbing life mass. Time slid by like watching a film in slow-motion. I was floating. We all were. On a great wave of sound I never wanted to end.

I was dancing rather well, although I say it myself. I kept visualising Sebastian . . . driving headlong from His thwarted rendezvous. I could imagine Him . . . materialising towards me . . . through the strawberry smoke . . .

'Well, hi there . . .' He'd say.

And I'd kind of look really cool and uninterested and say 'Hi'.

And I wouldn't even mention Jemima or anything until He did.

And then I'd be terribly mature and understanding about the way she'd let him down and He'd kind of put an arm around me and say something like:

'I can't think why I never noticed before . . . but you've got really amazing eyes/legs/lips . . .' and He'd kind of put His finger under my chin and tilt forward a bit . . . turning His head slightly . . .

That's when I tripped over Piggy.

'Piggy!' I said, coming back to earth with a jolt.

He was sitting on the floor all by himself, still holding his can of lager, or a very similar one.

'Did you manage to get through to that Simon guy?' I shouted in his ear.

He opened one eye: 'Not exactly. But don't worry, it's all under control. He'll find it.'

'How?' I asked.

'No hassle,' said Piggy.

'What do you mean—no hassle?'

'I've fixed it—that's all.'

I decided I'd have to leave things like that. I couldn't get any further response out of him so I headed off into the centre of the marquee where all the action seemed to be.

I hadn't noticed how hot it was until I felt a faint breeze on my face. All of a sudden I was dancing in an area with less of a crush. Then, with a shock that hit me like a blow on the head, the sound was turned off. In the silence that followed I was virtually deafened by the ringing in my ears.

A boy next to me with long dreadlocks dropped whatever he was smoking and exclaimed: 'It's a raid, man.'

I stood where I was like some real mal-co, still dazed by the music. People were pushing past me in a frantic rush to get to the exits. I heard the tearing of canvas as someone slashed a hole in the side of the marquee. Everyone began to spill out through it. I looked around for Jason or anyone else I knew. All I could see was a mass of backs pressing to get out, so I followed them. Outside, all these sound-blasted people were stumbling across the muddy fields into the darkness.

The cold dampness hit me like a wet sponge. Everything was rutted, mud-clogged and soggy, in fact, callously rural. I followed the crowd automatically as it headed towards the brightly lit road. Under arc lights a fleet of pick-up lorries was in action and I caught sight of a car being swung into the air like a toy to be carted away.

This was ser-i-ous, man. I picked up speed and stumbled headlong towards the bit of road where I thought the boys had left the car. I had to dodge dazed, phased-out party-goers who couldn't seem to understand why their cars weren't where they had left them.

I thought I knew where ours was. But when I reached the last parked car I still hadn't found it. Systematically I worked back, thinking I must have missed it, which was pretty impossible considering its colour. But I soon had to face the fact that it definitely wasn't there. Then it gradually dawned on me that I hadn't the faintest idea where I was. And since I had left my coat and keys and everything in the car, I was stranded.

I made my way towards the lights. With any luck, I might find someone who was friendly enough or stoned enough to lend me a fiver. And there were loads of policemen. If the worst came to the worst, they'd probably give me a lift back to London.

But the police weren't the kind of jolly approachable street corner policemen you saw in the daytime. They were frisking a boy and with severe expressions they were taking down things in notebooks. I realized with a sinking feeling that they were arresting people.

'Justine! Over here!' a voice shouted out of the darkness.

I swung round and a camera flash caught me full in the

face. I was dazzled for a moment and then as my eyes cleared I recognised Mike, the photographer who had come to Daquise with the famous Kathy.

'Please,' I said. 'Don't! I'm not meant to be here.'

'Not to worry,' said Mike. 'But since you are, luv, give us a quote. What d'you think of all this police brutality?'

Mike's attention had attracted a little crowd of people who obviously thought they might be missing a celebrity or something.

Mike continued, thrusting a pocket recorder towards my face: 'I heard some bloke say they've been planting stuff on people. Got any comments?'

A policeman was staring hard at me. Then I realized he was looking at my 'Organiser' badge. He intervened, taking me by the arm.

This produced even more enthusiastic flashes from the cameras.

'Out of the way now, you're causing an obstruction,' he said to the photographers and then added, 'This way Miss.'

The gaping interior of an open police van loomed ahead of me.

Then, by some miracle, my policeman let go. He had stumbled into a body that had fallen drunkenly at his feet.

I started running. It wasn't until I was out of range of the lights that I risked a backward glance. The 'body' held aloft a single lager can, skilfully keeping it upright, not spilling a drop.

Piggy was such a star!

I kept running, my heart pounding, wondering desperately what to do. Until out of the darkness I heard: 'Oh poop, I think I've trodden in a cow doo–doo.' It was a Chelsea accent I'd recognise anywhere. It hadn't changed one bit since our junior school days.

'Cinders!'

A group of figures were crowded around a BMW. One of them, a male, was saying: 'Hurry up Lucinda. You'll get us all in clink.'

Cinders . . . or rather Lucinda . . . turned and caught sight of me.

'Gosh . . . Justine! . . . I say, this is awfully, you know, THING, isn't it? Do you think we'll get our money back?'

'I've no idea,' I said. 'But you couldn't possibly give me a lift into Town, could you? I've kind of lost everyone. And my coat . . . And money . . . And keys . . . And . . .'

Lucinda brushed her hair out of her eyes and peered at my badge.

'Gosh,' she said. 'Won't you be in for it? You're one of the organisers.'

I hastily removed the badge. 'I just sold a few tickets.'

'I say, Nigel, can we squeeze another in? I think Justine's about to be arrested.'

Nigel leaned out of the car and eyed me.

'What if we're stopped?' he said. 'You don't have any *stuff* on you, do you?'

'No I do not,' I said.

'Don't get your knickers in a twist,' said Nigel. 'I only asked.'

Space was found for me and I squeezed in. I sat in the back wedged between one very large sleeping male who reeked of tobacco and snored loudly and a very thin girl who had to have the window open and kept on saying she wanted to be sick, but wasn't.

The conversation revolved between them, totally ignoring my presence. It was mostly about what substance produced what effect and how brilliant/mind-blowing/absolutely un-real it was. And it was very, very boring indeed. At last the conversation tailed away from sheer force of tedium.

By the time we hit the outskirts of London, I realized the

driver and I were the only two people left awake.

'Where do you want to be dropped off?' asked Nigel.

'Oh anywhere,' I said.

Anywhere but home, I thought. By now Jemima would be buzzing round her room like a wasp trapped in a jam jar: one place I simply couldn't go was 'home'.

'What's the time?' I asked.

'Four-thirty.'

'Anywhere central will do,' I said.

In the end he dropped me at Piccadilly Circus.

18

It was very cold indeed at that time of the morning and I didn't have a coat. I suddenly felt exhausted and very, very hungry. Boots was open. Its lights shone in a welcoming fashion. I felt in my pocket. If I had only had a few coins I could have bought a tube of throat sweets or something. All I found was Jemima's Pill.

I slipped into Boots anyway—just for the warmth. I stood by the Aramis display breathing in the faint but delectable smell of Sebastian. But I don't think All Night Boots takes kindly to loiterers.

The girl behind the Prescriptions counter was eyeing me with suspicion. She cleared her throat.

'Can I help you?' she asked.

'Not really . . .' I replied, feeling really embarrassed. 'Only looking . . .'

I turned on my heel and swept out with as much dignity as I could muster, which wasn't much.

I made my way miserably down Shaftesbury Avenue. An electrical goods shop offered a flickering display of television screens. I pressed against the glass trying to feel the benefit of the faint warmth from the lights inside. Most of the programmes being shown looked foreign. Then one screen in particular caught my eye.

There was this room which was in the most frightful mess. It was simply buried in half-finished plates of food and toys and books and a feeding bottle . . .

And there was this poor harrassed woman in the centre surrounded by children . . . three of them at least. Honestly, it was like the worst excesses of 'The Sound of Music' . . .

Then the woman grabbed the youngest, a baby, and thrust it towards the screen. It was screaming, its face puce with rage, although I couldn't actually hear it through the glass. And 'the woman' was trying to mouth something at me through the screen . . .

With a shock, I recognised Juste!

Oh my God . . . a baby!

This was getting totally out of hand. I mean, as far as I could see she wasn't even wearing a wedding ring or anything. Children! . . . Three of them! And they weren't nice fresh-faced 'Sound of Music' children, they were horrid and cross-looking. The eldest, a boy of about nine, appeared to be trying to poke a toy gun in her ear. Nine! I started to count back . . . Nine years and nine months took one back to . . . round about now!

Juste was getting even more frantic.

I cupped my hand over my ear and placing it against the glass I just managed to catch what she was saying:

'*For God's sake go home!*'

But how could I go home, for goodness' sake? I frowned and shook my head.

Juste kept bawling at me as if I were a moron and pointing at the baby. She seemed to be saying something that looked like 'pyjamas' over and over again.

I strained my ears to catch it between howls from the baby.

It wasn't 'pyjamas', it was:

'. . . JEMIMA'S . . .'

Why on earth would I want to call a baby of mine 'Jemima', for heaven's sake?

A baby! . . . Children! . . . *Three of them!* It simply didn't bear thinking about – so I put the thought right out of my mind.

I turned my back on the window and started to head aimlessly towards Leicester Square. There was no way I could go home in view of the fact that my keys were touring Britain somewhere in the Mafia car. I couldn't get in even if I did. And unless she had managed to carve her way out of her room with her Epilady, Jemima couldn't let me in either. With a shudder I pictured Jemima waiting behind the front door, ready to chop me into small pieces and turn me into steak tartar in the Magimix.

This vision was so chillingly vivid that I hadn't even noticed where I was going. I had ended up standing in the street, staring at a poster which showed this massive hot dog simply oozing ketchup. I can't stand hot dogs normally, so you can judge how critically malnourished I was. I was just standing there, my mouth watering, when I noticed this hand-written sign:

JUNIOR ASSISTANT REQUIRED
APPLY WITHIN

My brain started to make some lightning and pretty fundamental connections between the hot dog, my rumbling stomach, my penniless state and this offer of employment.

Beneath the notice was an OPEN/CLOSED sign showing the hours of opening. I was in luck. It said OPEN 7.00—4.30 DAILY. My watch told me it was six-thirty. I wondered how much a Junior Assistant earned. However little it might be, it could just keep me from terminal malnutrition. I banged on the door.

After a minute or so, a man in a greasy apron opened it.

'We don't give no free handouts here . . .' he said and was about to close it again.

'Actually, I wanted to ask about the job,' I said with dignity.

He studied my dirty, crumpled clothes doubtfully.

'All right, you'd better come in,' he said.

'How old are you?'

'Sixteen and a half,' I lied.

I don't think he was convinced by this but he didn't pursue the matter further.

'You got a proper place to live? I don't want any trouble, you understand.'

I didn't think that Cheyne Walk was an appropriate address in the circumstances, so I gave him a fictitious one in Hammersmith.

'Telephone number?'

He nearly caught me out there. But luckily I knew the Hammersmith code because it was Chuck's. Chuck's number kind of tripped off my tongue too, I think, quite convincingly. At any rate, he noted it down in a little red book.

'Previous experience?'

I shook my head.

'I can't pay more than £15 a day with no references.'

Fifteen quid! This wasn't enough to keep me in taxis. Clearly it was slave labour.

'I'll take you on trial if you want to start today,' he said.

He had risen to his feet and was putting rashers of bacon in a big iron pan. My mouth watered as an irresistible fried bacon smell rose from the pan.

He looked up expectantly.

'OK. I'll take the job,' I said.

He passed a plate with a bacon sandwich on it over the counter and shook my hand with his large warm one.

'I'm Mario, welcome to the shop. You want a coffee with it?'

He brought me a milky coffee and a doughnut as well and sat down with a cup of coffee himself. He shook his head as he watched me wolf down the food.

'You just work hard and we won't ask any questions, eh?' he said.

I did work hard. I had to. It was a positive culture shock. I mean, I didn't think anyone ate white bread any more. You would simply never believe the number of people who want Cheddar Cheese and Onion sandwiches. To the freshly-initiated sandwich maker, a Cheese and Onion is a real nightmare. For a start, onion rings are murder to cut, and once in the sandwich they cause havoc with the bonding of top to bottom. I was starting to have grave misgivings. I mean, would £15 stretch to Cabochard soap to neutralise the onion smell?

After an hour or so I felt as if I had done more than a fair day's work. Lack of sleep was making me taut and prickly all over. I slopped tea over yet another freshly-made sandwich.

Mario frowned: 'You want to sit down for a bit?'

I nodded gratefully.

He handed me a copy of *The Sunday Rag* and another coffee.

It would be *The Rag*!

My hands shook as I opened the paper. There was nothing on the front page—this was devoted to the latest mutant virus food scandal. There was nothing on the next couple of inside pages. But there it was on the fourth page:

WILD CHILD JUSTINE EVADES ARREST IN ACID ORGY

It was a pretty unmistakable picture of me. The way my

hand was raised it looked, most unfortunately, as if I was about to hit the policeman. It seemed there had been a real riot with masses of arrests. But apart from mine, there were no pictures and no names. Why did I always have to hog the limelight?

'Better?' said Mario.

'Not much,' I said, hurriedly slopping coffee over the paper.

'You wanna be more careful,' said Mario with a frown.

'Sorry,' I said as I tore out the page and shoved it in the bin.

Mario didn't seem too pleased. He took the soggy remains of the paper and put them over the radiator to dry.

I'd rather not go into the rest of the day. Enough to say, it passed—like a long exhausting nightmare. But at last Mario closed the door behind the final customer.

'Now we clear up,' he said.

I did an absolute mountain of washing up, without gloves too—I dread to think what was happening to my hands. Then I had to slop down all the work-tops while Mario washed the floor. At last we both slumped down at a table facing each other like two exhausted wrestlers.

Mario gazed at me with a half smile. 'OK,' he said. 'I reckon you'll learn.'

'In that case,' I ventured, 'do you think I could have today's money right away—I'm a bit short of cash.'

'Short of cash, eh?' said Mario and he pursed his lips and leaned forward so that he could take a wadge of notes out of his back pocket. He peeled off a couple of fivers and laid them on the table.

'But you said fifteen pounds,' I said.

'Fifteen when you're trained. You're only on trial, like I said. So you get ten, see.'

'I see,' I said with great restraint.

'Can I go now?'

'Sure. You go now. Come back tomorrow at seven o'clock sharp. OK?'

'OK,' I said.

19

I set out from the sandwich bar with no clear idea where I was heading. It was now totally apparent that I couldn't go home ever! My latest starring role in *The Sunday Rag* had well and truly settled that. I wondered if Mummy would always, in future, refer to me in the past tense, like she did about that Aunt of ours who went batty and collected cats. I supposed, gloomily, they'd give all my things to Jemima. At least I was wearing my Cons. But where was I going to sleep for God's sake? I mean, you hear things about people living in cardboard city. What no-one tells you is where to get cardboard at five-thirty on a Sunday afternoon.

Eventually, I found myself walking in the direction of Charing Cross station. I had some sort of impression there would be a nice warm waiting room with big comfy benches to bed down on. There wasn't.

Charing Cross wards off would-be dossers with a wide cold expanse of bare floor. And as for getting a nice peaceful night's sleep, the bright lighting and constant loud announcements from the speakers rule that right out. I soon found there were no benches either—comfy or uncomfy. The only available seating is in areas where you have to pay for things, like the Burger Bar.

I decided to try to gain inspiration in the Ladies. This cost 10p. But 10p well spent, because there, among the various posters about unspeakable diseases and Aids and things, I came across a message that seemed directed by some hand of fate towards me.

NOWHERE TO SPEND THE NIGHT?
The Women's Fellowship Association
offers sympathetic help and advice.

Under that it gave an address somewhere in the King's Cross area. I hastily memorised it and headed for the Tube. A whole 60p of my precious hard-earned ten pounds went on the half-price Tube fare!

I had to search through a maze of streets which looked like something out of the seedier bits of a third rate detective movie before I found the right address.

'WFA HOS EL' it said in insecure lettering over the door. It looked frightfully run-down. I rang the doorbell and waited what seemed like an eternity before a woman opened it a crack and without giving me a moment to open my mouth, said:

'Sorry, we're full.' And closed the door in my face.

Did she realize I had spent a whole 60p being lured to her measly hostel! So much for sympathetic help and advice. I rang hard on the doorbell again.

She opened the door a slightly wider crack. 'Yes?'

'Could you please give me some idea of anywhere else I could go?'

'Well, at this hour . . . on a Sunday too . . .' (It was only six-thirty for goodness' sake!)

She pursed her lips. 'You could try the Charing Cross Hostel,' she said.

'But I've just come from there!' I took the address anyway.

On the way back I dodged through the Tube ticket barrier without buying a ticket. Well, frankly, the frustration was enough to bring out anyone's criminal tendencies.

The Charing Cross Hostel was just as run down as the WFA, if not more so. However, it did have a door which let you in and a small mahogany booth with the reassuring word 'Reception' printed over it. An arrow pointed to a bell and said RING. So I rang.

'Can I help you?' The pinched face of a miniscule woman peered up at me from under the counter.

'I'm looking for somewhere to stay.'

'Room nineteen. Eight-pounds-fifty. Money in advance, if you please,' she said.

I handed over the money with some relief. I even forgot to enquire whether it was with bath or with shower.

It wasn't.

It was with several other beds however, and all of these were occupied. Room 19 was a kind of dormitory and, un-hardened by the rigours of boarding school life, I wondered if I would ever get any sleep in it.

I went in search of a bathroom to change in for the sake of modesty and then remembered I hadn't anything to change into anyway. But I could kill for a shower.

Then I realized there wasn't any soap and there weren't any towels. I headed downstairs to complain.

'Soap and towel 75p plus £1 deposit for the towel,' I was told. Since I only had 80p left I bought some soap but had to do without the towel.

As there wasn't a shower I had a bath, in spite of the ominous brown age patches and permanent high-water mark. I thought the soap might ward off the worst diseases. It smelt like something I dimly remembered as Lifebuoy, which was meant to give you all round confidence or ever-lasting inner cleanliness or something. Then I dried myself inadequately with my T-shirt.

Back in bed, practically fully dressed, with my wet T-shirt hanging like a limp ensign on my bed-rail, I started to ponder on my present situation. Then I decided to leave pondering until the morning. The cracked clock on the peeling wall told me it was nine-thirty p.m. Approximately thirty-six hours since I had last slept. I was just dozing off when I noticed 'The Voice'.

'So I said to him—what if she did? I wasn't going to worry myself about it, not likely. What with all that had gone before. They'd been carrying on and she knew it. That was the point, he said. And then we went through it all over again . . .'

There were sympathetic murmurs from the next bed.

'What did she say?'

'Well, she said it wasn't her fault . . . well, after all it was him who got her into it in the first place . . . If only people would be more careful, she said . . . She didn't specify who . . . but it was too late by then, wasn't it? I said, try the DHSS. But she said, well she couldn't, because of, you know . . . Say, have you got a light?'

'The Voice' continued for most of the night. But it wasn't that that kept me awake.

What kept me awake was a MEGA-CRISIS OF CONSCIENCE. Actually, I don't think I'd be overstating the facts when I say my whole life passed before me—like it's supposed to do when you jump off a cliff or something.

It started with me picturing Chuck standing outside the school being stood up, with all his friends filing by, bringing home to him, once and for all, what a wally he really was.

Then I kept on thinking of Jemima locked in the house, pacing back and forth like a caged tiger, becoming more and more savage by the minute.

And then I pictured Sebastian waiting at the Heathrow Air France check-in looking adorably lost and vulnerable. I lingered for quite a time over that.

And then I kept on thinking about Juste. Waiting desperately for the money, possibly facing a prison sentence! I kept picturing her wild-eyed and wild-haired with those frightful children and that dreadfully ugly baby which for some unaccountable reason she had called Jemima!

What would Juste do in a situation like this? I wondered.

The answer came back crystal clear as if Juste herself had spoken in my ear.

'Frankly, darling, you wouldn't find me hanging around in a fifth-rate doss house. I would have got myself a glitzy little suite in the Savoy and I'd have been on the blower right away to some darling little editor in Fleet Street.'

She would, too.

'After all, Justine,' I could hear her saying, 'There's no such thing as bad publicity!'

Those words took me right back to where it had all started. 'Mouse.' That's what she'd called me. 'Mouse!'

I mean, if it hadn't been for Juste I would never have ordered that Bacardi and Coke at the Ball. I would never have tripped up or had that picture taken. I would never have had to call *The Rag* to clear my name. I would never . . .

As my memory tracked down through all the other things I would never have done . . . and this took quite a time because there were an awful lot of them . . . it began to dawn on me that I didn't want to end up like Juste. I mean, she had quite obviously made an absolute mess of her life (which was my life as it happens). And she was going to go on messing it up, because she would simply never learn!

That's when I became aware of 'The Voice' again.

'. . . *I would never have left if it hadn't been for that. I mean, all I had were the clothes I stood up in and a ticket to London. But there you are, as I said at the time, who'll care anyway. Well you can't go on for the rest of your life, can you? . . . Can I borrow your matches again?*'

There was a rattle of matches and more sympathetic murmuring from the neighbouring bed.

That's when the solution hit me. The way out for Juste and myself was simple. I only had to change my name and my identity, then none of the things that had happened to Juste had to happen to me. It was so blindingly obvious! Having solved my problems, I should by rights have fallen into a deep, dreamless sleep.

But I lay awake for hours and hours trying to think of a suitable new name for myself. It's not that easy you know. I'd always wanted to be called something incredibly romantic like Juliet or Camille, with a surname like de Havilland or Pendrake, but frankly, I couldn't see myself starting a new life somewhere anonymous like Palmers Green with a name like that. I tried out more democratic versions like Vera or Sheila or June with surnames like Simpson or Wilson or Wilcox. But there are limits—I mean, can you imagine making anything of your life with a name like Vera Wilcox . . .?

'Oh blast, I've run out of fags . . .' said The Voice.

And then the lights went out.

The next day I woke up as soon as it got light, wondering where on earth I was.

'The Voice' was leaning over my bed saying: 'You haven't got a cigarette you could lend us, have you?'

I shook my head.

'Never mind love,' said The Voice. 'It's never as bad as you think.'

It was though. It was six-thirty on a Monday morning. And I didn't even have enough money to buy breakfast. There didn't seem to be anything for it but to haul myself out of bed and trudge to Mario's.

Mario was busy doing something to the espresso machine,

crooning gently to it as he did so.

'Oh so you came back?'

'Yes,' I said.

'You want brekkfuss?'

'Yes please,' I said.

'Better hurry now. It's a Monday morning, you know.'

I didn't realize the full significance of this comment until some hours later.

First there was the early, early crowd. Roadworkers and railwaymen who all wanted hot bacon and eggs which tended to glide off the grease as you passed over the plates. Then there was the early crowd who settled for thick, curling bacon sandwiches. Then came the first of the late crowd who wanted nothing but beakers of coffee delivered into their shaking hands. They were followed by the late, late crowd who were willing to grab anything and simply threw the money at you and ran. Then we got heavily into the Elevenses crowd and when that started to die down a bit Mario said:

'Now you take over for a while.' And he whipped next door to buy a newspaper.

I was having a bit of a battle with a beef and coleslaw bap when, out of the corner of my eye, I saw him standing outside reading it. Then he folded the paper, hastily consulted his little red book, headed down the road and disappeared into a telephone booth.

Typical! I thought resentfully. He was probably placing a bet or something, leaving me to do all the work.

That's when I started to realize that I wasn't exactly cut out for a career in catering. I think it must have been the start of the early, early lunch crowd. Queues built up outside as I worked my way through mountains of well-marged slices, shoving in fillings, slamming on lids, slicing, wrapping and slopping coffee into beakers.

The espresso machine became aware that a total incompetent had been left in charge and it hissed and fumed and glowered at me with its single red eye. Orders seemed to become more and more complex as I struggled on . . . shoving, slicing, wrapping, slopping coffee . . . Espresso or Cappuccino? Shoving, slicing, wrapping, slopping . . . Espresso or Cappuccino?

Then someone came back complaining that he'd got Ham and Mustard when he'd specified Branston Pickle. And a whole load of people joined in with complaints:

'I said white not brown . . .'

'Call that a portion of cheese—it wouldn't feed a sparrow . . .'

The espresso machine belched furiously as if it was about to explode so I turned on a tap to release the pressure. I watched in frozen horror as coffee poured out, spreading in a thick dark slick that soaked into the piles of cut bread. I turned to get a cloth and I think I must have caught the tray of coleslaw on my cardigan button, and the huge builder who'd come in to complain about his brown bacon sandwich slipped on it and fell . . . Anyway . . . It was lucky Mario reappeared when he did.

He was quite nice about it, actually. He helped the builder up and gave him his money back. Then he turned the Open/Closed sign to Closed and we both cleared up—very quietly.

When we'd finished I thought it was only fair on him to say:

'Frankly, I don't really think this job's quite me.'

Mario's big face crumpled, he looked for a moment as if he was going to cry. But instead he kind of tried to laugh.

'Frankly,' he said, 'nor do I.'

I didn't have the nerve to ask for any money. Well, it was barely half a day's work anyway.

As I walked out into the street a cab approached. It approached very slowly like a vision out of a former, happier existence. As if in a dream, I watched it draw towards the pavement and come to a halt.

20

The door of the taxi was flung open.

'Get in,' said Chuck and grabbed me by the wrist.

'What on earth are you doing here?' I said as he forced me down on to the seat beside him.

'I might well ask you the same thing,' said Chuck.

'You've absolutely no right to interfere . . .'

'Look. When you've stood for hours in the cold, waiting for a girl to turn up for a dance and she doesn't . . . Then waited the whole of Sunday for her to ring and apologise and she doesn't. And then some mad Italian wakes you up at some unearthly hour on the first Monday morning of the holidays to find out if you know anything about a Sloaney girl with multi-coloured hair who's positively causing mayhem in his sandwich bar . . . Not to mention this . . .' he thrust a newspaper into my hands. 'I figured you might need some sorting out . . .'

I read the headline:

ACID-HEAD RAVER MISSING

The 'Daquise' photo of me was printed underneath — thankfully with the rest of the Pack cropped off.

'Oh boy . . .' I said.

'I've come to take you home.'

For a wally, Chuck was being almost masterful! But there was no way I was going home.

'Thanks for the thought,' I said, 'but you can let me out now.'

'Sorry,' said Chuck. 'No deal.'

'Stop the cab!' I called out to the cabbie.

The cabbie, who was trying to negotiate the traffic at Hyde Park Corner at the time, slid open the dividing window and said, 'What's going on?'

'I'm trying to take this girl back to her home,' said Chuck.

'But I don't want to go home,' I said.

The cabbie slowed down a bit and said, incredibly unhelpfully, 'Look, I'm a family man myself and I've got a girl not far off your age . . .'

'Will you stop the cab, or shall I jump out?' I said.

The cabbie, spotting a policeman, swerved to the inside lane.

'How's about asking this officer to sort out where you do or don't want to go?' he suggested.

I had a flashback vision of Friday night's open police van.

'No, it's OK, drive on,' I said.

The family-man side of the cab driver totally took over at that point and there was absolutely no way of stopping him. He really put his foot down and we steamed into Cheyne Walk at one hell of a lick.

I was frantically trying to work out plausible and convincing excuses to placate Mummy, Daddy and Jemima as we speeded towards 122. But before I had worked out a single excuse—even an implausible or unconvincing one— the cab drew up.

Actually, Cheyne Walk was looking pretty busy for a Monday morning. There was quite a crowd outside our house. It had that static, expectant look of a crowd witnessing an accident.

When Chuck forced me out on to the pavement I noticed that quite a number of people were holding cameras. There was even a man with one of those big fluffy boom things for recording sound. How on earth had the Press found out where I lived?

All was revealed as Chuck dragged me up the steps. In Piggy's inimitable handwriting—in Day-Glo spray paint on the wall beside our neat brass 122—his message to Simon read:

JUSTINE DUVAL LIVES HERE

Chuck and I had a little battle on the steps when he tried to ring the doorbell. This was duly recorded with a wildly enthusiastic flashing of cameras. When the doorbell rang, a kind of shriek came from above and I looked up to see Jemima leaning out of her bedroom window. Actually the funny thing was, she didn't look angry at all—she had this kind of seraphic smile on her face.

'Hi there! . . .' she called.

And then behind her . . . Sebastian appeared . . . wearing *my* bathrobe!

My brain started making lightning connections . . . bathrobe . . . bedroom . . . baby . . . 'JEMIMA'S . . .' Oh my God! Suddenly, everything took a mind-blowing clarity . . . a boy of nine . . . Oh my God! Those children weren't mine, they were . . . JEMIMA'S! *Three* of them! Personally, I'd never have seen *her* as the earth mother type!

Just at that moment the Volvo drove up and Mummy and Daddy climbed out. Mummy was holding a copy of *The Rag*.

It wouldn't have been so bad if the Press hadn't taken that

awful picture of Mummy getting out of the car brandishing *The Rag* like a truncheon. It wouldn't have been so bad if Daddy hadn't found the envelope with the four hundred and fifty pounds in it on the doormat and I'd had to explain about the Energy tickets. It wouldn't have been half so bad if Mummy hadn't come across The Pill in my pocket and assumed it was mine. It wouldn't have been nearly so bad if Jemima hadn't had the portable with her in the bathroom. It seemed the whole experience of having Sebastian shin up the drainpipe in his climbing gear with a bottle of champagne in his back pocket and half a side of smoked salmon between his teeth had forged some kind of eternal bond. (The outcome of which became apparent much sooner than Mummy would have wished.)

It wouldn't have been anywhere near so bad if Juste hadn't come through during the ten o'clock news, interrupting a report about the Energy party arrests and accusing me, bitterly and tearfully, of 'RUINING HER LIFE'.

'Look,' she'd said, 'thanks to me every single thing you asked for in the letter has come true. And what have you done for me in return? NOTHING! You couldn't even stash away a small and essential sum of money to pay a fine for something that was ALL YOUR FAULT. Now I'm faced with a Prison sentence. What have you done with my life—you've ruined it!'

Actually, I was speechless.

I mean, who precisely did the ruining? And *whose life was it anyway?*

I hope I didn't come over too strongly. But I made a few pretty direct observations at this point.

I told Juste, to her face, that I thought she had been behaving in a pretty immature way, considering her age. I also said that I thought her attitude was selfish to say the least. I mean didn't she care about the havoc she wreaked on anyone . . .

Chuck . . . Jemima . . . Mummy and Daddy . . . Me?

I tried to point out, and I think I managed to without sounding too self-righteous, that fame and fortune were no substitute for the things that really matter.

'Like what?' she asked in a kind of subdued voice.

'Like getting somewhere, doing something, sorting yourself out!'

'You know what the trouble with you is, don't you?' she said. It came out like a kind of snarl . . .

'What?'

'You're getting middle-aged . . . and boring!'

So that's why I was standing on Albert Bridge at dawn the following morning, staring down at the river.

I had decided to end it all.

Earlier in the garden in the dim morning light it had been hard to find the right place in the flower bed. I had started digging frantically with my bare hands until at last I had felt the shiny surface of the bottle. The letter was still inside. With relief I had uncorked the bottle and taken it out.

Now, standing in the centre of the bridge, I ripped the letter into shreds and let them fall, one by one, down into the river. I leaned over the parapet and watched the tiny scraps of paper floating—bright specks against the blackness, shifting, changing places—all those fragments of my wilder dreams and lost ambitions, slowing sinking out of sight . . . forever.

Seriously, thanks to seeing how Juste had turned out, I had come to realise, with the kind of maturity you can only gain through *real suffering*, that the things I had wanted such aeons ago when I'd buried the bottle simply weren't what I really wanted at all.

In fact, I had made an eternal and irrevocable vow—that when I was Juste's age, I wasn't going to be in the least like her. No, she was going to be somebody totally different.

SHE was going to be like ME.